CW01209098

Agnes Wanjiru

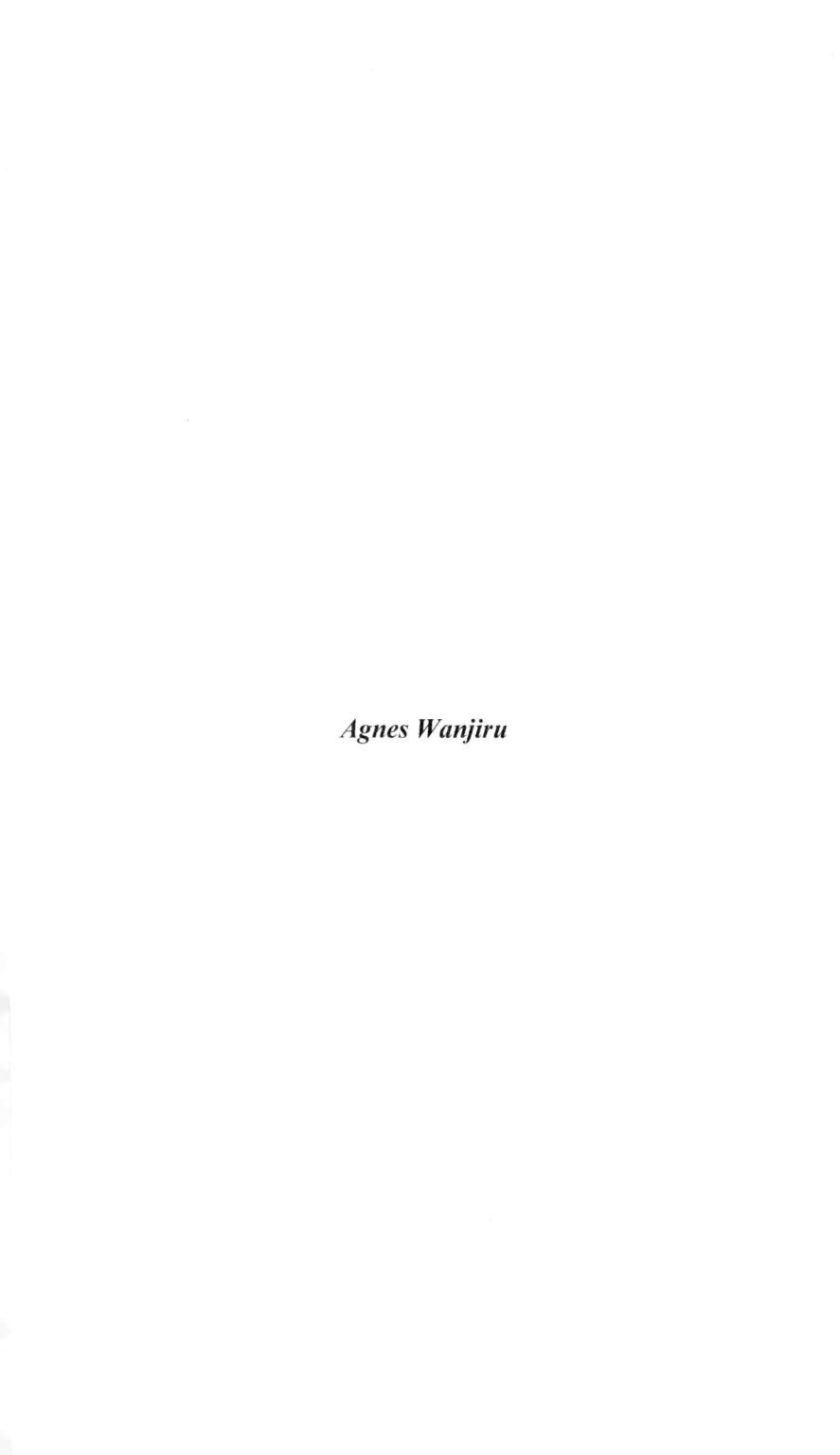

Also by Onia Fox:

Covid Blues And Twos (Jessica Taylor)
Lockdown Erotica

Listless In Turkey (Jessica Taylor)
Travel Suspense Thriller

Enemy Closer (Jessica Taylor)
Procedural Suspense Thriller

Alexa – humorous coming of age, short story

Connecting Doors

by

Onia Fox

Jessica accepts a work assignment to India, far away from her husband, as she works through recent trauma and evaluates their marriage.

A young work colleague catches her eye, a dashing hotel concierge wraps a protective arm around her shoulder, and she forms a close friendship with the au pair staying in the adjacent hotel room. A horrendous crime of international significance occurs behind locked doors. Jessica's friend appears secretively and unexpectedly to offer emotional support – seen by some as an aggressive stalker.

The police detectives spread wide the investigation net.

Contents

Chapter One 1
Chapter Two 7
Chapter Three 18
Chapter Four 38
Chapter Five 49
Chapter Six 60
Chapter Seven 76
Chapter Eight 85
Chapter Nine 91
Chapter Ten 121
Chapter Eleven 140
Chapter Twelve 150
Chapter Thirteen 164
Chapter Fourteen 177
Chapter Fifteen 186
Chapter Sixteen 201
Chapter Seventeen 214
Chapter Eighteen 241

Chapter One

Jessica lay back against his hip, her breathing now recovered. He continued their love making for a while longer than she needed, and he now panted in the heat of the tiny twin room. The ceiling fan whirred noisily overhead. Jessica smiled at the part it played, the squeaking keeping time with her rhythm when they started, her on top. The blade ripping her dress from her and tossing it across the room as she fought to pull it over her head, with the zipper jammed, to allow him access to her. She was not averse to a little spontaneity, but this had all been a little ... desperate.

Still, it scratched an itch.

She closed her eyes and drifted back to the first time she made love to her then future husband Jason, on the Italian beach. A similar temperature with the sun on her back, but dry and fresh in the sea air. She dozed for a couple of minutes. The bedroom door creaked, she awoke and glanced, realising it had remained open to the outside corridor.

'Shit. Does nothing work in this room?'

Jessica padded over and managed to locate the catch, on the third attempt. Kneeling on the rough, thin blanket, she studied his gorgeous open smile, before nodding towards the side of his face.

'Your ear is, you know, pouring blood.'

He reached for a tissue.

'That will be because you bit it, Jess.'

'Umm. And that will be because you weren't gentle with me when I asked you politely. They are not your office stress-balls.'

'Sorry. Look, may I ask something please? Was I ok? Did you enjoy it?'

'What? What sort of question is that?'

'I mean you were great, I guess …'

'You guess? Anyway, I am not asking. Not polite.'

'Sorry, it doesn't matter.'

He continued to gaze at her naked body, his eyes drinking in the sight. His hand trembled as he reached to stroke over her breasts.

'Shit! Are you a virgin Sumer? I didn't think of that one.'

'Me? A virgin? Of course not. That is so funny. Me? Ha!'

'You can tell me …'

'I said no! On my mother's life, I am not a virgin. Goodness me Jess. You English.'

Jessica concentrated on running her fingers through the tight curls of his chest hair, matted with sweat and goodness knows what else – his aim was poor.

'Ok Sumer don't be defensive, I'm only asking. So, what about before this afternoon? Were you a virgin this morning?

He shrugged and looked away.

'Shit, shit, shit! I should at least have bought you flowers and, and, I don't know, kissed you or something. Sorry.'

'Don't apologise, Jess. Not polite.' He grinned wide. 'And neither is keep saying *shit!*'

'Look, walk me back to my hotel please; let me buy you afternoon tea. This should be a special day to remember not just a …'

'*Just a* what? I have had the most surprising and wonderful day. Thank you.'

'Please don't say *thank you*. Not p…, oh forget it.'

She turned over onto her back again and noticed a crossbow and bolts proudly displayed above his desk. On the desk stood a Lynx Africa deodorant and an oversized framed photographed of, presumably, his parents – keeping watch over his bedroom antics. Jessica was desperate to make an inappropriate joke about impressing his mother or the accuracy of which he could shoot his bolt – but resisted; this was a first and possibly only date.

Boys will be boys.

*

They left his hostel in the *modern* main town of Fort Kochi and walked the baking hot streets to the historic spice market, turning left along the road running parallel to the Arabian Sea and the edge of the Kerala Backwaters, towards Jew Town. Most people who could afford the few pennies for an autorickshaw, and there were crowds of people around them who could not, would not have braved the heat of the afternoon, but Jessica loved the walk. India was everything promised: exotic, hectic, a genuine assault on the senses.

The hotel, a beautiful colonial white building, stood behind a high wall against the shoreline, surrounded by mayhem, a ferry slipway, and Chinese Fishing Nets. An oasis of serenity, calm, coolness, and cleanliness. The concierge approached the couple; an imposing, tall Sikh dressed in traditional military Raj uniform. He wore a huge, belted holster with a long-nosed revolver and an ornately carved ebony nightstick *for decoration.* Jessica liked military paraphernalia and previously asked if the ancient pistol was real and loaded, he carefully avoided answering.

'Mrs Taylor! Welcome back to Branston Wharf. I hope you have had a splendid day, so far.'

'Thank you, Mr Singh. Like you, I have been working. Now my colleague and I are ready for tea.'

Singh escorted the couple across the shady courtyard and opened the heavy plate-glass doors into the cool, airy foyer. Jessica walked Sumer to a low, heavy, dark wooden table and couches, beneath manually operated wooden punkah fans. Jessica had operated the fans by pulling hard on the ropes, under the supervision of the receptionist. But thankfully they were now only for show, Branston Wharf Hotel no longer employing punkah wallahs.

'You sit and relax Sumer. I just need to pop to the room.'

She called across to reception for afternoon tea and skipped up the grand staircase to her room, quickly washing herself and shaking her head at the mess. Returning to the lobby, she slipped a smartly bound, mass-produced, complimentary hardback book across the reception desk and whispered to the receptionist. The book had sat with a copy of the bible, Sikh Guru Granth Sahib, Koran, and Vidas in her hotel room desk. She took her seat next to Sumer and poured them both fruit juice as the waiter appeared with an impressive display of tiny sandwiches and pastries on a silver tiered tray with a matching tea pot.

'Jess, this is lovely. Thank you.'

She beamed back.

'You know I am married Sumer? And please remember I am still Mrs Taylor in the office.'

'Absolutely Jess.' He opened his mouth to say something clever to reassure her of his discretion. Jessica giggled as his mouth gently gaped like a stranded trout.

The receptionist appeared with a beautifully gift-wrapped parcel, tied with red ribbon, the paper having a diagonal pattern, repeating the words *Branston Wharf Boutique Hotel*.

'A parcel for you sir.' She smiled at the couple and returned to her desk.

'For me?'

He opened the gift to find a copy of Salman Rushdie's novel, Midnight's Children, set in the exact area they now sat having tea. He opened the cover to read the handwritten inscription.

My dear Sumer,

Thank you for holding my hand and showing me such a wonderful time in Kerala. Love Jess x

Sumer turned the book over in his hands, several times.

'Jess …' She placed a silencing finger to his lips.

'Drink up Sumer, I have Teams video meetings this afternoon, sorry.'

She hugged him a goodbye, but avoided a kiss, and stood with the concierge watching him disappear into the ocean of humanity outside the hotel gates.

Chapter Two

Jessica closed the bedroom door, leaning back, eyes closed. Lideri spoke. She sat cross legged on the bed, watching Jessica.

'What have you been up to Jess? You are looking ... fatigued.'

Jessica snorted a laugh.

'I am certainly not telling you, Lids! Get those dusty clothes off my bed, you shouldn't even be here.'

Lideri lay back onto her elbows.

'*I want to talk to you about some things.*'

'Not today, Lids. I'm running late. You need to go, I have calls to make.'

Jessica set her laptop on the desk and opened Teams video conferencing. She nodded towards the door, but Lideri smiled sweetly, laying back on the pillow. Jessica released a long sigh.

Jessica took deep breaths as the laptop connected. She had no doubt she loved Jason and he loved her. But things were not good between them, recently. She requested a transfer to the job in India, to give them time apart; Company jumped at her offer. She longed for these catchups and then dreaded him picking up.

'Hey Bambi! How are you doing? You look lovely, glowing.'

'Thanks, Jace, you are looking kind of hunky yourself. I think this sun suits my skin.'

Jessica was quarter Afghan on her father's side. Any hint of sun turned her skin olive, whereas the long UK winters gave it a slightly jaundice hue.

'Missed you last night. Date night.'

'Same. What did you do?'

Jessica's stomach tightened as he described his evening. The long soak in their double bath, with a glass of wine, listening to Jessica's favourite Joy Crookes album on Spotify. He chose Jessica's favourite dopiaza instead of his usual takeaway curry, he even played an episode of Married At First Sight in the background as he read the newspaper. In bed, he slipped her pillow under the duvet and switched on her side of the electric blanket, to feel the heat. She managed to keep most of her tears in check, but her heart cracked.

'Next Friday, we will synchronise Jace. We will have a Teams bath together. I'll see if chef will make me a dopiaza on room service and you can grab a jalfrezi as usual. We can both light candles. We will fall asleep in bed together. I might even let you watch me … you know. *Where's the soap?*'

Lideri snorted a laugh from the bed and Jessica blushed. She crinkled her nose into a smile and watched Jason reply with his lopsided grin.

'*Yes, it does, doesn't it!*' They laughed together. 'When are you coming home Jess?'

'Soon. We have a last-minute push in the office, then I will be on the first flight back, honest.' Lideri scoffed again. 'Here, I will give you a tour of my room. When I gave up my flat in Chennai to set up the satellite office in Kochi, I insisted they put me in somewhere a bit posh. Trish, from back in the Portsmouth office, found me this gem.'

Jessica walked her laptop around the room, giving Lideri time to reluctantly scurry out of the way. She showed him the huge, high fourposter bed, and the massive panelled ensuite. She pulled open the heavy louver doors onto the shared balcony with a view to the pool and the Arabian Sea beyond. Back inside she peaked behind the heavy curtain, which covered a locked and bolted connecting door. She then continued out into the expansive corridor and over the balustrade to the foyer below.

'Oh, I must tell you this funny story Jace. On my first night here, I decided to stand on the balcony and watch the busy harbour for a bit, before going to sleep. As you know, I don't wear anything in bed, so I pulled on the shortest of T's, which I had worn during the day and closed the door after me, to keep the bugs out. You've guessed it, there is no handle on the outside, it automatically locks.' She gave a long, embarrassed laugh – as much for being so scatty as for finding herself half naked in the shared space of a hotel.

'Never a dull moment with Jessica Taylor, as your old dalliance once said. Then what?'

Jason joined in with her laughter. He realised, early into their relationship, that it was physically impossible not to laugh along with Jessica – her giggling being so infectious.

'I had to walk along the balcony, past all the other rooms to the end, back onto the landing, down the stairs to reception, thankfully no customers were there, back up the stairs with the receptionist and stand on the landing while she used the spare key to open the main bedroom door. There is an ordinary night-latch and then a big key for an ancient mortice, as a kind of a fob – luckily, I hadn't used the big mortice lock and left the key in the keyhole! I spent the whole time stretching the T over my lady bits, which meant my top kept popping out.'

She laughed louder at herself. Controlling her giggling, she studied her husband's face, emitting light with his own laughter. She really did love him, but this is where the conversation normally deteriorated. She would ask about his friend Priti, he would ask how she was managing without sex, she would lie, then become defensive. This is the first they had laughed together for a very long time. She decided to quit, whilst ahead.

'Darling, I have to shoot, sorry. I have a Teams meeting with the company shrink.' She rolled her eyes. 'I'll call you later and arrange date night – with a time-difference. I promise you won't be disappointed.' She crinkled her nose as she smiled and watched her husband's expression, as his heart melted.

'Be good Jess. And stay out of trouble. I know neither is an easy ask. Love you.'

He smiled and winked before ending the Teams video call, deciding not to give her the time, and pressure, to reply an *I love you too*. He knew in his heart, however they eventually ended-up, that she did love him.

*

Jessica walked to the heavy louvered balcony door, opening and wedging it with a chair – at least she was fully clothed this time. The breeze blew the warm air through her hair. After her hooking up with a colleague at lunchtime, she needed a long soak in the tub. Probably with a bottle of cold pinot.

A junior colleague in my team; what was I thinking?

Walking back into the room she took a beer from the mini bar, sitting in the comfy desk chair, in front of the laptop.

'Ok Lideri. You have five minutes. What gem of lifestyle advice have you thought of, for me today?'

Following a brief silence, Jessica turned to see the bed empty of Lideri. She walked to the open door and looked both ways along the balcony, before returning to her desk.

Everyone who mattered: Jason, her friends Cath, Peter, Stacy and Trish, her brother-in-law, her boss and best friend Amara, and her colleague Onslow, all said the same. Lideri was bad news. She never was a proper friend. She sucked the life from Jessica, she was a control freak and a stalker of huge proportions.

Jessica was in therapy following the recent events in Turkey. She had been dragged into a major military mire resulting in a Russian jetfighter being shot down by Turkey, and then kidnapped by Kurdish fighters. All this happened in the shadow of her shooting whom she had believed to be a terrorist wearing a bomb vest. Company referred her for a mental health assessment and straight into therapy. She contracts to Company as a consultant; her boss and friend Amara made it clear to Jessica that therapy was a condition of her continued employment with Company. Amara argued against Jessica covering the Indian project, but with no alternative, senior management overruled her.

All the while, Lideri wangled her way deeper into Jessica's affections – even following her to India.

The Teams meeting connection screen appeared; Jessica *accepted.*

'Hey Mrs Taylor. Good to see you again, although I preferred meeting you in person when you worked here in Chennai. Drinking early?'

'Hi Rani. How would you know what is early, you don't drink?' Jessica was good at answering the therapists' questions with questions. Both her therapists were accomplished at ignoring them. 'No, not early. I am having a beer, mid-afternoon, on a hot day, after work.'

Rani touched a button on her keyboard, adding a marker to the recording of the conversation.

'We advise you to work no more than five-days per week, no overtime.'

'I just popped in. A few of my team are working. No big deal.'

Lideri scoffed from the sofa, making Jessica jump. She glared at her.

'Are you alone Jess? These consultations are private unless you prior request someone to sit in for support.'

'I am alone. My balcony door is open: you can hear voices from the pool, and the ferry stop next door. You'd be amazed what drifts in through that door.' She glared again at Lideri.

'I have a couple of points from our last session, or would you like to talk about something else? Anything happen this week? Or anything worrying you? Have you heard from Lideri?'

'Go on. What points from last time?'

'You were having vivid dreams.' Rani let the statement hang.

'Yeah. Same. Really odd. Some feel like hallucinations – like they might be happening in this room, or I might be back in England or Turkey. Odd. Apparently, my malaria tablets can cause dreams.'

'You think you are hallucinating?'

'No! I didn't say that. I know they are dreams when I wake up. I am just saying they are very real, at the time.'

'And you obviously remember them?'

Jessica nodded. *Why on Earth did I mention hallucinations?*

'Rani, I need to level with you here. May I speak candidly, without you running back to management?'

'Nothing in these sessions goes anywhere, except your notes, which may be reviewed by other clinicians – including Dr Cindy Stockholm of course. I am really her eyes on the ground, while you are here in India. Tell me what is worrying you?'

'The only *condition* I have is *Real Person Condition*. I am doing these sessions to keep my job. If anything, they are making things worse.'

'*Things?* So, you accept you have these *things* to address?'

'No. Look, I had a shock in Turkey, and it has put a strain on my marriage. The sooner you sign me off, the sooner I can get back to developing my career and concentrate on my marriage. I will say whatever it takes, to tick the boxes. I just need time out, a minute to myself, break up with myself and make up with myself again. Maybe I'm going crazy, or so narcissistic and twisted because I only talk to myself. Come on girl, I need out of this weekly mirror talk.'

Rani and Dr Stockholm seldom discussed ideas for discharging her, but Jessica kept it to the top of the agenda.

'What dreams did you have this week?'

'I dreamt I hooked-up with a young man from my team at work. It was real, like it happened. Apart from making me a bad wife, is that a reflection of my mental health?'

'Dreaming it, or if you actually did it?'

'You know. If I did it, say.'

'What do you think Jess?'

'I mean if I am in India, does it matter? If he never knows?'

'You once told me how Jason and you have no secrets. Would it play on your mind? Would you always struggle with yourself to keep it secret? Would that put extra pressure on your mental health, and the relationship with your husband?'

Jessica shrugged. She glanced at Lideri to see her shocked expression.

'But anyway, it was just a dream.' She tried not to look at Lideri, who now slowly shook her head, disappointed in Jessica.

'Any other dreams, Jess?'

'Tell her about the other 'dream' *you had Jess, sleeping with the airline pilot the night you landed in India.'*

Jessica stayed focussed on Rani, but blushed deeply at Lideri's whispered comment, from only just off camera.

'I dreamt I shot somebody.'

'That wasn't a dream though Jessica, was it?' Lideri peered at Jessica from over the top of the laptop. Jessica felt sure Rani would hear her, but she showed no reaction.

'Let me finish!' Jessica shouted at Lideri, but Rani answered.

'Take your time Jess, there is no hurry.'

'Sorry. I was saying I dreamt I shot someone on the balcony outside my room, here. I was convinced it really happened. I ran back into bed and called reception. But then I realised the man I shot was actually the poor guy whom I really shot in Turkey.'

'A nightmare or a flashback? Or a fantasy?'

'Fantasy? God no Rani, why would you say that?'

'I am not *saying* anything, Jess. I am asking.'

'At some point it was a dream, I even ended up back in bed. But I really did call reception. They answered, but luckily I realised before saying anything. I don't want any of your shrink-shit Rani, am I mad or not? For once, answer me straight.'

'Firstly, we don't use the word *mad*. But, to put your mind at rest: no, I do not think your dreaming is a sign of psychosis. But we are working through other issues that I suspect are at play, not least your possible PTSD. I know Dr Stockholm is looking into some reckless decision making, and placing people on pedestals, as possible pointers to something left undiagnosed from before Turkey. But *mad*? No.'

'And the dreams?'

'I suggest we monitor them for now, Jess. We have discussed various coping mechanisms and cognitive strategies. Take a moment to think them through. They are like the flashlight in your toolbox – you don't want to be looking for the batteries after the car has broken down. And if you have any confusion between dreams and reality, just call my office for a follow-up chat. Ok? It sounds like Dr Google has warned you about vivid or bad dreams when taking chloroquine anti-malaria medication. If you are able to cope, I suggest we look again once you are home and finished the medication.'

'My fifty-minute hour is up Rani. Catch you next time. And thank you, I am indeed not mad. In fact, I am not even reckless – I just love life.'

Rani pointedly checked the clock over her shoulder, smiled and ended the Teams video call. Jessica stuck the black sticky-tape back over the laptop camera lens.

She glanced at Lideri, seeing her wide smile and twinkling eyes. Jessica straddled Lideri's lap, facing her on the sofa and sitting back onto her thighs.

'What are you smirking at Lids?

'Mirror Talk? *You just quoted lyrics from a Griff song to your shrink; it didn't even make sense! That is so funny Jessica, this is why I love you; you are just so funny.*'

The couple stared at each other, both studying the other's face. Lideri was several years younger than Jessica, but life was tough. Working outside in the mountain sun had darkened her skin and she had tiny scarlet pimples and liver spots on her forehead from the damage. Her many laughter lines etched with dust, dirt, and manual labour. She had a prominent *eastern* nose; more defined than her Kurdish heritage – perhaps Arabic or Persian. Jessica thought it unlikely she would age well; she was slim, her face a little gaunt. But her lips were full. Hair black, wavy and luscious. Her body sexy, if not slightly girlish. Jessica fell into her clear, huge eyes whenever she saw them, even as they bickered.

They both snorted a laugh. Lideri, the much stronger of the two women and a born fighter, allowed Jessica to pin her wrists against the sofa and squirmed her face away as Jessica playfully tried to force a kiss onto her lips. Still laughing, Lideri turned her face into the sofa, so Jessica buried her own face into her friend's neck, nibbling at her ear until Lideri could no longer breathe through laughing.

Chapter Three

Warned off going into the office on a Sunday by occupational health, despite Sumer and a few fellow engineers in her team working through the weekend, Jessica stayed in bed for an hour longer than normal. She exchanged a few texts with Jason, made herself coffee from the room's Nespresso machine and listened to music on her smart speaker – including *Mirror Talk* by Griff. Pulling on her thin summer dressing gown, she wandered onto the shared balcony to watch the cruise liner MS Queen Elizabeth power past just yards away, on her journey to Kochi port.

She could not remember dreaming during the previous night, but her belly sunk every time she saw something unusual, such as the cruise ship disproportionately filling her view, wondering if she was, in fact, still asleep. Leaning against the balustrade, cradling the steaming first coffee of the day, she idly watched a young family, frolicking by the pool.

Still early, she guessed the parents gave up coaxing the tots to sleep another hour and had instead brought them to tire around the pool before the heat of the day. Perhaps the tired children would then nap, so the couple could enjoy a grown-up lunch together. Or they would sneak back into the sack and make another brother or sister.

Jessica liked to people watch and often made-up backstories and future scenarios for strangers, to entertain herself. He was mid- to late forties, well groomed, confident, handsome. She was much younger, pretty, less assertive. They held their adoring children's attention equally. The children were beautiful, all curls and symmetry. Jessica guessed the family Mediterranean, although the young woman was unusually tall.

Mum grabbed the children's hands and mock ran along the side of the pool, all three squealing; dad walked behind groaning, arms extended like a zombie. Once caught, he tickled his partner's waist, and she theatrically fell to the floor laughing. The children tried to tickle away their father, but he ran his fingers over their bare chests until they also lay on the floor giggling. Mum jumped-up and became the zombie as dad grabbed the children's hand and the game repeated in the opposite direction. This time mum consensually pushed dad into the pool, as the children laughed hysterically. She lowered them into his safe hands, joining them in the water, but staying back to allow dad to interact directly.

Lideri seemed to pester Jessica on difficult days and often left her alone on good days; this was a good day. She was happy, slept well, and looking forward to breakfast, but for some reason Lideri appeared, uninvited as always.

Well, nearly always.

She stood behind Jessica's shoulder, liking to make an entrance. Jessica decided to deny her that satisfaction and spoke as if she were expecting her.

'So, what do you reckon? I think he is a young industrialist, rich but very private. She is his trophy wife; I mean she must be half his age. I'm not feeling sympathy for her, I mean he's gorgeous. I'd do him. And her. Or both together.' Jessica laughed at her own inappropriate thoughts. 'What do you think?'

'Actually, he is my husband, and she is our au pair. But yes, they make a striking pair. I have done him, but she is a bit young for me and a bit ... female.'

Jessica spun around bringing her hands to her mouth.

'Sorry, sorry, sorry. I was just fooling, I thought you were my friend, stood there!'

The woman smiled, genuinely amused. She gently prised Jessica's hands from her face and the two women giggled together.

'Oh, I am so sorry. I feel so foolish. Please forget everything I just said. It is obvious they are not together. In fact, I assumed she was his daughter, honest. Not that he looks old enough to be her father, obviously. Maybe a stepfather or a big brother.'

The woman's giggling turned into a belly laugh. Still holding Jessica's hands, she replied.

'This is so funny. I could watch you dig this hole all day, but you are probably already deep enough. Let me introduce myself. I am Diaz Anderson, Mrs Taylor. The hunk is my husband, Cameron. The children are Gregory and little Nadia. The trophy au pair is Zeynep.' She winked at Jessica 'The guy stood in the shade is Troy, he works with us as well.'

'Please call me Jess. But you already know who I am?'

Diaz held a folded piece of hotel headed paper.

'I am working my way around the hotel guests, apologising for any nuisance and reassuring them that everything is ok.' Jessica raised an eyebrow. 'You haven't been for breakfast yet?'

The women decided to head for the breakfast room together. Jessica wiped her face with a damp flannel, brushed her hair, gargled with mouthwash, pulled on white linen high waisted trousers with a sun-washed effect linen, baby blue tunic. She double checked she had the room key and left by the balcony, pulling closed the door by the louvers.

'This room next to you is the children's and Zeynep's. And Cameron and I are in the adjacent room, on the end.'

The couple walked onto the landing and were confronted by an Indian soldier, sat on a chair, cradling an INSAS assault rifle. He smiled and wobbled his head at Jessica and, on seeing Diaz, stood and saluted. Before Jessica could speak her surprise, they reached the top of the stairs with a sightline along the front of the rooms. Soldiers similarly sat outside the two neighbour's room, at the far end past Jessica's room, and the near end close to the top of the stairs. As the couple walked into view, there was a Mexican wave of standing, saluting, and sitting soldiers. They saw others in the foyer, at the front door and the rear entrance to the pool area.

*

'I'll have the pancakes and scrambled egg please.'

'I'll have the chef's special breakfast, please, with a side of extra yogurt.'

'Jess! You are not having the curry for breakfast? Nobody, western, has curried breakfast.'

Both women laughed.

'I do. Every so often I need a whole week off curry. I actually have to supervise the chef, because he can't help spicing my Heinz Baked Beans on white sliced toast, or my poached eggs. Mostly though, I am a curry three-times-a-day girl. But there is an elephant in the room – well twenty elephants with machine guns.'

'Yes. We are the Canadian High Commission to India. *We* – listen to me, how pretentious. My husband is the High Commissioner. But I can assure you, I work equally as hard. In some ways, so do the children – it isn't a normal life. Security is especially visual, ever since the 2008 Mumbai attacks, and then our own government kindly stirred the pot by siding with the farmer protesters in Delhi. But it is nothing to worry about, honest!

'I guess it is an occupational hazard. We were posted to Turkey back in 2004 when our Canadian government decided to acknowledge the Turks genocide against the Armenians! Cameron sweet talked his way through that particular diplomatic incident, but we were certainly ready for the promotion to India. Turkey and Canada are still barely talking.' Diaz rolled her eyes. 'Politicians eh! Who'd 'ave 'em?'

'I'm glad you walked me down, it would have startled me, following a thing that happened, recently. Anyway, I don't mind a few good-looking soldiers for decoration.' The couple laughed again. 'So, tell me what an obviously highly intelligent and motivated High Commission First Lady does to keep busy.'

Despite the Atlantic divide, Jessica enjoyed chatting with this attractive, elegant, clever, and interesting woman - in her own native tongue. She explained a little about the High Commission and her own contribution. She spoke passionately about her work with an AIDS/HIV foundation, which she worked with before meeting Cameron, whilst they both worked in Africa. She championed the foundation in the consulates she moved around on marrying Cameron and was now their ambassador. She amused Jessica with various anecdotes, some quite risqué, but avoided anything to do with official policy, or security – even avoiding saying when they would move from the hotel. Diaz loved India as much as Jessica, but they were expecting a change in deployment. She tapped her nose conspiratorially, although it was well known newspaper gossip.

'I thought your husband was speaking French to the children and he looks kind of French. Same as, um, people do. From France, I mean.'

Diaz laughed at Jessica's ham-fisted attempt not to speak about her husband and the pretty au pair together.

'He is French-Canadian, the children will be bilingual like Cameron. Zeynep is Turkish, although she will soon have her Canadian citizenship.' Diaz showed Jessica her crossed fingers.

'Turkish? She is unusually tall for a Turk.'

'Yes, and legs that go all the way to the floor, lucky moo. Mind you she needs them, chasing my two around all day. Have I dragged you away from your friend?'

Jessica frowned, wondering if Diaz had seen her with Sumer, although that was yesterday, before the Canadian's arrived.

'Friend?'

'You said you thought I was your friend. On the balcony.'

'Ah yes Lideri. Sorry, my mind went blank. Um no, I am not seeing her today, I was still half asleep. My first day off work for a while; I slept so well.'

'Is there a husband or significant-other on the scene?'

'No. She will always remain single now, I guess.'

Diaz sat back with a grin.

'You, Jessica, not your friend. Are you married?'

Jessica giggled at herself and explained about Jason and the short-term assignment to India. She wondered if the reference to keeping Jessica from her friend was Diaz ending the breakfast chat.

'But I will let you get back to your family holiday. Thank you for putting my mind at rest and hopefully we will talk again.'

Jessica went to peck a kiss on her cheek, but Diaz pulled her in for a hug.

'Great to meet you, Jess. I am so relaxed with you, and I haven't laughed so much for a long time.'

*

Jessica returned to her room and retrieved her bikini. She dived into the pool and swam towards Zeynep, laid back on the concrete steps of the pool – her top half exposed to the sun, below waist in the water.

'Hey. Zeynep?'

The young woman sat and smiled but did not respond. Jessica saw suspicion in her eyes.

'Sorry. Diaz pointed you out. I am Jess. I am in the room next to you.'

'Of course. Mrs Taylor. Pleased to meet you. You could hardly miss our arrival; I hope we do not disturb or unnerve you.'

'*Memnun oldum Zeynep Hanim.*' She waved away Zeynep's concerns.

'You speak Turkish?'

'Not really. I have a small house in Turkey, well, more a shack, really. And I sometimes work in Turkey. I dated a Turkish soldier once, so I know lots of swear words.'

Zeynep raised her hand to her mouth and, wide eyed, gave a short giggle.

'This lot swear every other sentence.' She made an expansive wave towards the Canadian's rooms 'I am surprised the babies do not ask for their *effing* bottles!'

The pair giggled again.

'You have Sunday's off?'

Zeynep shrugged 'Sometimes.'

Jessica smiled to herself. Even the au pair was radio silent. Jessica previously nagged, cajoled and threatened her colleague, Onslow, to stop nattering about the job and anything secret, without success. This girl was a pro.

'You must do lots of travelling, with the Andersons. Do you enjoy it?'

'Yes, I love it. I was living on my uncle's tiny farm and looking at a life of picking tea. Diaz brought me onto a scheme she was involved with and *voila*!'

'They seem such a lovely family.'

'Yes. They do.'

Jessica smiled to herself again. *Clever.* She longed to ask about the scheme, and why or how Zeynep obtained Canadian citizenship – but the young woman gave her no way in. Her ex-partner, Chris, always tutted at Jessica's prying; Jason just thought it funny. She daydreamed about Jason again, before shaking her head and clearing her thoughts.

'Anyway, I will leave you to enjoy your day off.' Zeynep returned a smile, sweet, but noncommittal. 'And see you around, neighbour.'

They shook hands for the first time.

'Sure Mrs Taylor. *Gorusuruz.*'

'*Gorusuruz, Zeynep. Bana Jessica veya Jess.*'

Jessica floated to the opposite side of the pool, before powering a few lengths and climbing out at the diagonally opposite corner. Offering her new friend a final wave, she collected a towel from the trolley and padded towards her room, drying herself on the way.

*

Jessica napped during the heat of the midday sun, before pulling on her earlier linen trousers and tunic. She added a floppy sunhat and a silk shawl to protect the tops of her arms. Mr Singh hailed an autorickshaw to take her to the edge of the spice market.

On foot, the road took her over a bridge spanning a dry riverbed. Shacks clung to the banks, some no more than a couple of pallets and polythene sheets. She sat on a shady part of the armco barrier, taking-in the scene. A moving square of rag caught her attention, she wondered if a large animal was caught underneath, perhaps sheltering from the sun. The movement stopped, and a young couple appeared from underneath, walking back to the overcrowded shacks. The young woman smoothed down her sari with one hand, interlocking her lover's fingers with the other. Jessica casually averted her gaze, stood and continued her journey – now realising what she had just witnessed.

Further along the road she squeezed back against a broken gate, to allow a young woman to pass with a huge trunk of firewood balanced on her head; the woman's brown face baked almost black by the weather and sun. She dragged along a girl, perhaps six years old. The child was completely naked, with bare feet. She wore a piece of orange shoelace around her wrist as a bracelet and tugged on a length of string. Tied to the string was a stone, bouncing behind. This *toy dog* was likely to be the only toy the girl owned. Possibly the only object she owned. She would share her mum's sari to sleep at night, along with her mum's plate, mug and cooking pan, if mum had all those items. She would share her mum's patch of ground somewhere, as home, hopefully with shelter in the rainy season.

Jessica saw poverty on every trip out in India, but seeing this naked, filthy child dragging her stone dog for amusement, brought a lump to her throat. As often happened, a small group of boys gathered to watch Jessica in a mostly *local's* area. She turned away and covered her face as if she had dust in her eyes. Once the tears stopped, she sniffed loudly, slipped on her sunglasses, and continued her journey.

The road bent sharply to the right. There was little traffic on this section – clogged with porter's barrows and piles of sacking. She saw three lepers on the corner some days. Today a small crowd gathered around two of the beggars. As Jessica approached, the group parted to allow in a shopkeeper, holding a hessian sack. A council worker, wearing a blue uniform and cap, took and draped the sack over the corpse of the third beggar. The red flashing lights of a council ambulance blinked lazily in the heat, edging forward at walking pace. The flow of pedestrians squeezed past. Jessica crossed the road and turned left along a narrow alley, towards the waterfront, promising a row of bars and restaurants.

The alley and shop awnings offered protection from the blaze of the sun, but the air felt humid and oppressive. Coffee and tea shops lined one side, selling samosa in squares of newspaper. Rows of spice merchants lined the opposite side, their brightly coloured goods arranged in rows of boxes and drums. Each shop suspended a huge mirror on the back wall to reflect the produce to passers-by. The air heavy in spice, everyone, including Jessica, sneezed and coughed their way along.

Jessica noticed a broad-shouldered western man, sat on a table outside a café. He nursed a paper cup of cola. From the expression on his face with each mouthful, Jessica decided he must have laced it with something stronger. They nodded and smiled.

Between two spice shops opposite the café, stood an open gate into a busy wholesaler's warehouse. Smells, noise, and heat poured out from the opening. The far doors onto the waterfront also stood open – Jessica slipped inside and headed slowly towards the waterfront. Porters, customs, and stevedores jostled and shouted, dragging around sacks and barrows.

'Hey lady! My spices are cheaper than chips!'

A scrawny teenager sidled up to Jessica. His eyes red from the spicy atmosphere, his hands, and clothes filthy, his feet bare.

'I can do special deal on barge full of cumin.'

Jessica laughed at his sincerity and lay a hand on his shoulder.

'I love cumin, my favourite spice. But maybe not a whole barge.'

'For pretty tourists.' He produced a strip of empty polythene envelopes, spooning cumin into the first pouch, sealing it closed. 'What else, lady?'

Smiling brightly and gesturing, eyes wide, to piles of sacks and drums around her - she shrugged. The young man ran from piles of sacks to pallets of drums, spooning spices into the strip of pouches.

'I can tell you price. Or you decide; you tell me.'

Jessica thought hard, chewing her lip. It was a challenge. Eventually she decided he should name the price. Running the strip over a set of scales and scribbling numbers onto a pink striped paper bag with a tiny stub of pencil, he presented the package to Jessica.

'Last chance lady. Pay what you like.'

She smiled and winked, before turning over the package to see the price circled. 180 rupees. Less than two British pounds. She saw the business sense of his first offer, she would have guessed at much more. She took her going-out-for-the-day wallet from her leather shoulder bag and pulled out a 500 rupee note. The young man wobbled his head, calling out for assistance. An older boy took the note and, in a moment, had Jessica's wallet up ended, with coins and notes tipping into the first boy's open hands and onto the floor. Smaller boys scurried around collecting coins from the floor. Jessica stepped forward, grabbing back the half-emptied purse, whilst keeping her left hand on her bag, as the older boy disappeared into the shadows.

The tall man from the café opposite appeared to one side of Jessica and shoved the first boy against the pile of sacks. He sat winded, wearing a surprised and hurt look on his young face. The man put his left arm around Jessica's shoulder, holding his right hand out in front of her as a shield. He tugged her back towards the café. Nobody stepped forward to help the young man, as he struggled to stand.

'Get your fucking hands off me!' The man ignored Jessica. She swung her leg back, stamping him in the shin. 'Let go of me or I'm screaming for help!'

He stepped back, releasing her, shaking away the pain from his leg. She ran back to the boy, helping him to stand, and holding him upright against her chest. He bent double, Jessica thought he would faint, but he stood upright again holding the pink paper bag containing the strip of spices. He was too winded to speak but managed to smile as he handed her the bag. He pulled away and slunk into the shadows, following the older boy.

Jessica glared at the man from the café, with her best expression of contempt. She strode through the warehouse towards the waterfront, the sea of workers, pretending to have seen nothing of the commotion, parted in her path. Outside she glanced left and right, before turning towards the nearest waterfront bar.

'Kingfisher!' Jessica barked at the waiter and headed towards a table on the water's edge. 'Waiter!' The waiter turned to face her. 'Sorry. I didn't mean to snap. A nice cold Kingfisher beer please.'

The western man rested his hand on the back of the spare chair.

'Excuse me Mrs Taylor. May I join you, please?'

'No. Fuck off.'

He shrugged and sat at the neighbouring table, signalling for beer.

'I thought you were being mugged. I was only trying to help, sorry.'

Jessica played with her phone. She wanted to offload on Jason, but he would only tell her off for finding herself in *another situation*. The first boy trotted to the bar and checked with the waiter before going to Jessica.

'Hey lady. Your change. My brother swapped all your heavy coins for notes with our teller. We took money for the spices. Cheap as chips!'

He handed new notes and a couple of large coins to Jessica, turning to leave. Western man waved a 100 rupee note in the air.

'Hey boy! For you.'

The boy did not look around but flipped his middle finger.

'Wanker, Sahib!'

*

'How do you know my name?' Jessica spoke calmly now, ordering another beer. 'From the Canadian accent, I gather you are part of the team?'

'I work with the High Commission, yes. I saw you talking with my colleague on the balcony.'

'Ah Troy! The man in the shadows. Security?'

'Logistics.'

'Shall I sing you The Bodyguard song, like Whitney.'

'If you like, Mrs …'

'Jess, please. You had better sit here. The only two white people in the bar, talking on adjoining tables? We look like spies, plotters, or drug dealers.'

He shuffled over and sat in the next chair, taking Jessica's arm and rubbing her olive skin, mocking her self-description of being white. Jessica took the opportunity to scrutinise him. Everything about him was neat and tidy. His clothes tailored, but not flashy. His skin pocked and marked from younger days, but now grease free, clean-shaven, and moisturised. She watched his curious eye motion through the sides of his Ray Bans; when his head stopped moving, the eyes continued scanning. He clocked everything. He had chiselled features, big in every dimension, a physique heavy with muscle, but carrying little fat. She laughed.

'Jess?'

'Sorry, sorry. I was racking my brain, remembering where I have seen you before.'

'And?'

'Stan Smith in the *American Dad* cartoon. The hapless CIA hunk!' She continued to laugh. 'Sorry, rude.'

He scoffed and shrugged. 'Oh well. Better than Roger the ugly alien, I suppose.'

'So then, *Stan*, is that your background, CIA? Or did you go straight from work experience to human shield?'

He studied her face for a while before scanning the neighbouring tables.

'Provost.'

'Canadian?'

'Yes, of course. What did you expect ma'am? Korean? 3 Military Police Regiment.'

'How did you make the jump to …' She looked around for eavesdroppers. 'Blimey *Stan*, you are making me nervous!'

'I was ready for a change, not getting any younger. This lot were looking for someone and I had a contact on the interview board. Metaphorically speaking.'

'But you still get into fist fights protecting Canada's finest?' She gestured to a split on his lip, by touching her own.'

'Yes, something like that. I was headbutted by little Greg. Well, more like the nanny swung him at me.' He chuckled at the thought. 'She always carries her first aid pack, we all do,' he patted a bulge in his back pocket, 'so at least she could stem the blood. Luckily Gregory wasn't bruised, think of the paperwork. But to give her her due, she insisted I fill in the injury book – she is very professional, clever kid.'

'Day off from your dangerous work fighting tots?'

'I always have a good look around the environs. I am never off duty.'

'For provisions?'

'Sorry Jess?'

'You said you are in logistics.' She gave him a coy smile.

He laughed. 'You should join up. Intel.'

'One other thing Troy. You push your way into my business and manhandle me again, and you will never father another child.'

She stood and left, leaving the tab for him to pay.

*

Jessica walked a similar route back to the hotel. The dead lepper now gone, his two friends still in position. One lepper wore his dead friend's greasy cap. Mum, daughter, and stone dog had moved away on their journey through life. A family of pigs snuffled around the nuptial blanket – a new life, possibly, conceived. A cycle rickshaw pulled over for Jessica. The hotel stood too far away for a cycle rickshaw, but Jessica took it to the very edge of Spice Market, deciding to walk the remainder, the sun now cooling.

'Mrs Taylor! Welcome back to Branston Wharf. I hope you have had a good day, so far. Really, you must not spend your time walking through dust and heat. You must take less exercise and fatten yourself, for your husband. Keep my card and call if you cannot find a taxi – I will send one.'

Jessica laughed. In her Anglo-Saxon life, she was not used to such close physical and emotional proximity with strangers. She was barely used to Turks joining in private conversations at the bank or pharmacy – but Indians took it to a whole new level.

'So, my husband would like me to be fat?'

'Ah you modern girls. My daughters are the same. No man likes a skinny girl. I have been to England, Mrs Taylor, did I say?' The pair sat down outside Singh's security lodge. He glanced towards the hotel to check management was not watching. He poured a tea for himself into a copper cup and one for Jessica into a paper cup. 'In India, poor people are skinny and rich people are nice and fat. In England, rich people are thin and poor people are fat.'

Jessica laughed and nodded.

'England? Really? Where?'

'Birmingham, Southampton and London, obviously, but Leicester mostly.'

'I live near Southampton, not far along the coast. Chichester? Portsmouth?'

'I know of Portsmouth. You have a quarter called Spice Island, where spices from India were landed.'

'Yes, we do! Small world. Even now they have special permission to open the pubs for longer – going back to when the sailors needed watering … and servicing in other ways, although that industry has moved slightly further north in the city. Now it is fishing boats and bananas. Same shit, different century.'

'Indeed Mrs Taylor.'

'Mr Singh …'

'Please call me Gurdit, Mrs Taylor.'

'Then you must call me Jess.'

Singh glanced towards the hotel again and grinned.

'Thank you, Mrs Taylor.'

'What did you do in England? Holiday?'

Singh shrugged, topping the cups from a tea pot sat over a tealight.

'I was, I am, an academic. I visited some temples and spoke.'

'Spoke about?'

'Academia.'

Jessica scoffed, jutting her head forward slightly, encouraging him to elaborate.

'Sikhism. History. The future. Justice. Academia.' He suddenly jumped to his feet. 'Please stay and finish your tea; work calls.'

Jessica watched Singh walk to the empty gate and stand, alone. Her tea tasted stewed; she allowed it to run into the gutter, heading back to her room.

Chapter Four

Jessica woke and sat. She gave a long, luxurious stretch and yawned, smiling at Zeynep.

'Hey. What have you got there? And, um, how did you get in?'

Zeynep smiled and nodded towards the open balcony door. Jessica rolled her eyes at her own omission, of leaving the door open, allowing in the mosquitoes and bugs.

Unusually, she wore pyjamas. She slipped out of the high bed, onto her bare feet, and padded to Zeynep.

'Let's have a look.'

Zeynep unzipped her blue striped pool bag as the two women peered in.

'Nadia? Is she ok? Her lips are blue.'

'I'm not sure Jess. It's really my day off, but it feels I am always on duty. I think she might be dead. I don't suppose …?

'Sure. Give her here, you get off.'

Jessica pulled the limp girl from the bag and waved her limp arm to Zeynep, as she left through the open balcony door. Nadia wore an orange shoelace tied to her wrist as a bracelet.

'Let's get you settled young lady. If you are dead in the morning, I'll let your mum know.'

With a free hand, she opened the desk drawer, and took out the complimentary books. She brought Nadia to her face, sniffing deeply among the curls. Jessica adored the smell of babies' heads, although Nadia also had faint odours of raw meat. She laid her into the drawer and slid it closed. Eyes half shut, she slipped back into bed.

Although still tired, she could not drift off to sleep. Something worried her. She went through each family member and friend in her mind, trying to recall who needed her help.

'Shit! The baby.'

Jessica shouted out, running to the drawer. There were no handles, it locked automatically. She clawed at the drawer front but could not grip the polished veneer.

'Zeynep! Lideri! Help me!'

She fell onto her knees and screamed.

'Diaz!'

Jessica heard the banging on her door, but could not wrench herself away from the baby, locked in the drawer. The door opened and Singh burst into the room. He shone a torch around; the receptionist followed with an Indian soldier, turning on the main light.

'Mr Singh! Please open the drawer quickly!'

The receptionist pulled Jessica away and cradled her against her chest. She tried to cover Jessica with a throw from the bed, but Jessica pushed it away. Singh cautiously slid open the drawer, shining his light inside as he inched it open. The drawer was empty, the books neatly stacked on the desk. Troy entered the room, dressed, but feet bare.

'Troy, Nadia is ill, she needs help.'

Without speaking, he left the room, tapped on Zeynep's adjacent door, and held a mumbled conversation. Jessica heard the door open and close. She stood, but both Singh and the soldier signalled for her to stay in the bedroom. Troy returned.

'Good news Mrs Taylor, both children are fine.'

'You can't believe Zeynep, you must check. Zeynep is off duty.'

All eyes fell on Jessica, but the group relaxed. Singh smiled, the receptionist rubbed her hand up and down Jessica's forearm.

'I have spoken with Zeynep, she has everything under control. And I have seen both children. I had a good look; they are sleeping peacefully.'

'Troy, I wasn't dreaming. Mr Singh, I wasn't.'

'I know you don't need me to interfere Mrs Taylor, Jess, but why don't I sit for a while, until you doze off?'

Jessica nodded. Singh replaced the books into the drawer, and seeing Jessica staring wide eyed, turned a latch at the back and took out the whole drawer, placing it on the floor.

*

Jessica woke to the sun peering through the window, curtains pulled back. The small, carved occasional table had moved from in front of the connecting door and now stood near the sofa. A used coffee cup and half empty water tumbler sat on the table; scatter cushions piled one end of the sofa. Her pyjamas sat folded neatly on *Jason's* pillow.

Shit! Please don't tell me I did all that crap naked.

She retrieved her oversized *comfort* rugby jersey from the suitcase in the bottom of her wardrobe, sniffed it deeply, and pulled it on. She studied the dregs of coffee in Troy's discarded cup, finding his lip smears on the rim, smelling his tiger lip balm. She pressed the rim against her lips, before topping the dregs with a fresh shot of espresso. There remained a hint of bourbon, from the dregs.

From her perch on the balcony, she waited to see the children, to see Nadia.

The voice came from over Jessica's left shoulder.

'Jessica. Good morning. Fancy a curry? I hear you had a fitful sleep.'

Jessica turned to see Diaz.

'Good morning.' Jessica managed a cheery response. 'Sure. You go on, I'll catch you up.'

Diaz leant against the balustrade, her right shoulder in firm contact with Jessica's left shoulder.

'Work today? What do you do for that Company of yours?'

'I project manage. They are buying some bits off our Ministry of Defence.'

'The type 42 destroyer?'

Jessica turned to study Diaz and scoffed.

'You probably know more about the deal than I do. Let's eat breakfast, I'll get dressed.'

'No hurry. Let's wait a bit and ogle my husband and his trophy.'

Jessica turned to see the smirk on Diaz's lips. Zeynep appeared by the pool, waltzing with Gregory held in her arms, humming. Jessica tensed, standing to her full height, searching for Nadia. She waited an age until Cameron appeared, holding Nadia high on his shoulder. She sucked her thumb lazily. Seeing Diaz, she straightened and waved. Diaz replied, blowing exaggerated kisses.

The women looked at each other. Diaz pulled Jessica into a hug and Jessica sobbed with relief.

*

The courtyard was busy, with businesspeople heading out for the day. Jessica dialled her own office number.

'Hello. Mrs Taylor's office, may I help you?'

'Sumer! Hi. I have some reading to do here, but I will be in soon. All ok? Look, arrange a team-meet for ten. I want to know what we achieved for all that overtime I paid you lot over the weekend, yeah?'

'Sure Mrs Taylor. I will pop on the tea pot.'

Jessica had already rung off. She wanted a moment with Mr Singh, before her taxi arrived. He stood to attention, speaking with a slim, studious man in round-rimmed glasses and a brown, loose linen suit. A female colleague studied Mr Singh as the man spoke. Immediately behind stood a soldier – his assault rifle held at the ready. Mr Singh rested his hands on his gun-belt, the soldier tensed, and Singh moved his hands away from the holster and behind his back. The female handed Mr Singh a business card. They all took a step backwards, before the man and his colleague turned away. The soldier followed them towards the gate, finding his chair to sit on.

'Hey. Mr Singh, Gurdit. Do you have a moment?'

'Always time for you and everyone at the wonderful Branston Wharf, Mrs Taylor. I have ordered two taxis, to arrive shortly. You are the most important of my guests – your taxi is the second to arrive.'

He grinned widely but showed little humour in his eyes.

'Firstly Gurdit. Thank you for charging in last night, to save me. You are my hero.' He bowed his head, graciously. 'And sorry for the fuss. My malaria tablets give me nightmares – I dread to think what other side effects my poor little head suffers.' She looked to her side as she finished her speech. 'Also, sorry for my dress code last night; I probably did not meet Branston's minimum required attire.'

'I did not notice Mrs Taylor.' Jessica gave him a mock, disbelieving scowl. 'You are too skinny for my old eyes to see.' Jessica laughed.

'Who were your new friends, Gurdit? They looked quite serious.' Singh shrugged. 'Police officers look the same, world over.'

'They were checking security, because of our celebrity guest, perhaps. Celebrities like my beautiful and esteemed Mrs Taylor.'

They walked together to the Indian Ambassador taxi and Singh held open the door - saluting before returning to stand outside the security gatehouse. The engine spluttered and died; the key starter failed to turn the engine.

'One moment, Mrs Very Important Person.'

The driver produced a starting handle from under his seat with a flourish, jammed a piece of bespoke timber to depress the accelerator, and disappeared outside and under the bonnet line. Jessica idly gazed from her window, back towards the hotel.

Troy ushered Mr Singh into the doorway of the gatehouse. He seemed to talk sternly to the concierge and although Singh stood respectfully to attention, he showed a trace of defensive body language, with his weight firmly on the trailing foot and his forehead dipped slightly towards Troy. He took a business card from Troy, to add to his recent collection.

Troy gone; Singh caught her eye. She smiled and Singh mimed a clapping gesture as the taxi reluctantly spluttered into life.

*

Jessica had all but forgotten about her sweaty, quick, tryst with the junior colleague, just two days before. With her vivid dreaming and malaria tablets, she almost doubted it had happened. Sumer waited behind, after the meeting as usual, for instructions. His caste higher than most in the office and, although Jessica struggled with the whole situation, she found it easier to deal directly with Sumer and let him cascade to the others.

'Have you read Midnight's Children by Salman Rushdie, Sumer?'

'I have started reading it, Mrs Taylor. It is beautiful.'

'Yes.'

'Thank you.'

'Thank *me*?'

Their eyes met. He did not look away, nor wobble his head. He glanced behind at the general office.

'Yes, Jess. Thank you for the book. Are you ok?'

'Me? Sure. I hope you enjoy it.'

'Enjoy it Mrs Taylor? Not polite.'

Jessica blushed deeply, not sure if she regretted the inappropriate liaison, or was pleased that it had actually happened, and her mind was not playing tricks.

'Get back to work Sumer.'

Her voice was gentle, her smile pushed up her cheekbones and her eyes twinkled.

'Yes boss.'

*

Jessica sat towards the back of the following meeting, which she facilitated. She was the most senior manager attending, but all discussions and actions were for others. She ran through emails on her phone. A message appeared from Sumer.

'Sorry boss. You know the young clerk doing the charity pan-Indian autorickshaw challenge. She is running around for some upfront donations to pay her entrance at lunchtime. Do you want to chip in?'

'Of course, Sumer. Please take some notes from my bag in my bottom drawer, from the leather purse. Don't be stingy, but I don't want to show off, either. Yeah?'

'Yes Mrs T. Understood.'

*

Jessica could always find productive work in the office, reading back over reports and checking progress against the plan. Dotting *I's* and crossing *T's*, looking for anything which may affect productivity or profitability. The more resource and time she had, the more thorough the forensics. It was obvious to Jessica, and the office managers, that she could take her responsibilities back to Portsmouth to complete, or even leave the project and move on. She was delaying going home.

She spoke and spent less time with Sumer during the day than she had prior to having sex with him. It was a balance, she did not want people to associate them as a couple, neither make the gossipers think they had had a tiff or were trying to act discretely. As she came down the stairs, Sumer coincidentally fell into step from the next landing.

'See you tomorrow, boss.'

'You will Sumer. I can't believe you are all keeping me here, we need to finish up! Let's look at an exit strategy for me, tomorrow.' She stopped at the foot of the stairs and tested the weight of her bag. 'Strange. I am missing something. Shit! I brought my hotel keys with me this morning by mistake. Now they're gone.' She started to retrace her steps.

'The small keys attached to the heavy brass key with a steel ring was definitely in your bag when I took the collection money. Please wait.'

Sumer left Jessica at the foot of the stairs, sprinting towards the office. Jessica took a leather sofa under the air conditioning. He returned less than ten minutes later, jangling her keys for anyone to see – she wished he had not.

'They were in your drawer boss. Sorry, I must have …'

'Or I took them out Sumer. It doesn't matter. May I walk with you as far as your room? Then I can have my daily fix of the spice market.'

They walked together along the wide pavements of Kochi Main Town, Sumer buying them both a small polythene bag of frozen melon juice from a street vendor. Jessica turned it over, looking for the opening and straw. Sumer retrieved it, biting off a corner. Jessica still held the bag, his hands over hers. She accidently squeezed some juice over his nose; squealing a laugh and trying to catch the spurt in her own mouth. Still both holding the small bag, he purposely squirted some over her cheek. They both wiped the others face with spare hands, giggling together. Still holding hands and the bag, Jessica kissed him lightly on the lips.

'Are you popping in Jess? Break your journey?'

Her heart pounded; she could hear blood coursing through veins in her ears. Her hands and chest felt clammy. She glanced down at her own chest to check for signs of her … anticipation, lust. She nodded vigorously. They walked another hundred yards to the corner. Jessica stopped, taking a step towards Sumer; she stared towards the ground.

'Actually Sumer, I had better head off.' He nodded a reply. Without looking up, she mirrored his nodding and walked on, towards spice market.

Chapter Five

Jessica arranged to meet Sumer, and others from her office, at the cricket ground across the road from her hotel. The sun dropped; the land-breeze picked up. Chef approached Jessica in the foyer, menu in hand. He spent an hour each early evening, talking through supper options and preferences with guests in the foyer and around the pool. They stepped back towards the row of low tables and couches to allow soldiers to pass, leave the foyer and climb into the back of an army lorry, which then drove just fifty yards to the cricket ground, parking again.

The Andersons arrived in the foyer with Zeynep and Troy. The entourage stopped to talk with Jessica.

'Goodness Jess! You always look scrumptious, but really?'

'Thank you, Diaz, and likewise. Quite a trophy.' She winked and smiled. 'You are leaving us?'

'No. We are taking the children to look around the pimped-up autorickshaws doing the charity challenge.'

She held Nadia in a baby sling across her chest. In a long white cheesecloth dress, laced at the front and wearing leather beaded slippers, Diaz reminded Jessica of a has-been-hippie. A short, small, bodice-busting jacket added an intense burst of deep reds, blues, and greens. The jacket matched some of the colours in Jessica's short, strappy, summer cotton dress.

'May I join you?'

The women linked arms and continued towards the gates. The remaining soldiers gathered in the courtyard, *ready*; the warrant officer scouring the cricket ground and area outside the gates.

'Cameron was invited as guest of honour by the mayor. We managed to convince him to allow us the honour of enjoying the evening with the children instead. I mean Jess, there will be speech, after speech, after fucking speech!'

Jessica laughed, squeezing Diaz's arm.

'First world problem.' Diaz stopped to study Jessica. 'Sorry Diaz, just messing. I am not lecturing.' Diaz squeezed Jessica's hand.

Police halted traffic as the group reached the road. Troy stepped forward until he led the group, continually visually sweeping the area around them. Cameron, clutching Gregory for validation, greeted the mayor with an outstretched hand. A charity volunteer joined the group to explain about the challenge and point out some of the parked tuk-tuks, outlandishly decorated by participants from around the world.

Small groups of smiling locals and foreigners, mostly of university age, proudly gathered around their own self-decorated vehicles. Children ran from tuk-tuk to tuk-tuk, honking horns, ringing bells, or stroking the yards of pasted fabric, stuffed toys or plastic elephant tusks cable tied to the rickshaw handles.

Cameron did not allow Gregory to run around, holding his hand firmly. When the child became impatient as his father talked with participants, Zeynep stepped forward. Jessica now saw Gregory was tethered to Cameron. Gregory wore a harness, visible through his Canadian Oilers ice hockey polo shirt. A thin, plastic coated wire tether, snaked through his sleeve and attached to Cameron's wrist by a fake watch bracelet. Troy stepped forward, discreetly removed the bracelet using a magnetic fob, and reattached the bracelet to Zeynep's wrist – adjusting it to fit. Troy maintained an equal distance between Zeynep with Gregory, and the rest of the group. When Zeynep moved too far away, Troy brought her attention to something closer to the group and she immediately complied.

They found the autorickshaw crewed by the young woman from Jessica's office. The group spent some time with her. Diaz produced a complimentary bag of goodies from a sack carried by one of the hotel porters and gave it to the young woman. It contained small bottles of Clearly Canadian and Canada Dry drinks, maple syrup centred chocolates, Canadian maple leaf decorated baseball caps with Canadian and Indian flag insignias, ice hockey shirts with *Canucks* and *Jets* names emblazoned, *Dalhousie* and *Simon Fraser* University hoodies, and a stuffed toy grizzly bear in a scarlet Canadian Mounted Police uniform. The young woman immediately added the toy to the base of a fake whip aerial, with a sparkle coated cable-tie.

The young woman was delighted that her senior manager from halfway around the world, had made the effort and found the time to attend and wish her luck. The fact Jessica arrived with one of the most important foreign diplomats in India was a double honour. The young woman beamed so much that her wide grin prevented her speaking clearly. Other competitors gathered around and, as Jessica kissed both cheeks and gave her a good luck hug, laughed as the woman forgot to let go. Sumer stepped from the group and gently eased the woman away from Jessica.

The Andersons made their way back to the hotel following a parade of the pimped autorickshaws around the cricket ground, to the applause of charity workers, supporters, and dignitaries. They planned a late picnic supper with the children, on the shared balcony outside their room. Zeynep, Sumer and Jessica crossed to the ferry boat slipway and walked along the narrow walkway between the hotel wall and the Arabian Sea.

With Jessica in the middle, one arm through each of her friend's arms, the three walked to the base of a rickety wooden jetty, which led to one of the huge Chinese Fishing Nets. Fishermen lowered the war-machines-of-nets into the ebbing tide and scooped out passing fish. The loads now a fraction of those for previous generations, the fishermen encouraged tourists to join in operating the ropes and pulleys and make a small monetary contribution.

The fishermen played to their crowds, having teams of girls trying to operate one side, whilst a single fisherman easily operated the other. Or adjusted the mechanism so that a seemingly hunky man was only able to move one side a fraction of that of a woman on the opposite side. Jessica and Zeynep laughed at the shenanigans as Sumer returned with beers.

Encouraged by the women, Sumer stripped to his waist and asked to operate the nets. Jessica and Zeynep cuddled close, watching – his muscles stretched by the effort, his torso glistening with perspiration in the setting sun. Jessica was pleased the fisherman made Sumer look the strong hunk as he, with a little discrete help from the fishermen, hauled in an impressive load of fish. The fishermen made a big show of refusing the rupees Sumer offered – but then took them anyway.

As he returned to the women, Jessica noticed his frown, looking over her shoulder. She turned to see a small mongrel dog, part whippet, with four puppies in tow, slink along the gritty beach towards them.

'Quick, quick.' He ushered the women onto the jetty, standing between them and the dog.

The dog snarled in his general direction, his arms now outstretched to corral the dog and brood towards the hotel wall. As each wave lapped against the shore so the dog, looking evermore disorientated, spat a snap and growl at the sea. A policeman appeared, a local man leading the way to the dog. A small crowd gathered in a semicircle behind Sumer. The policeman gently and quietly ushered the crowd further back. He slipped on a facemask and latex gloves from his belt pack.

Troy appeared, trotting down the beach towards the policeman. He flashed an ID card before pulling out his mobile phone. Jessica watched the Andersons move from the balcony back into their room, closing the heavy door. Troy nodded to the policeman. He drew his revolver. A puppy tried to latch onto his mother's teat and only just succeeded, as the mother snapped at her offspring. A shot rang-out, the mother's neck exploded as she fell back onto the wall. The puppies all froze for a moment, before the hungry puppy tried to suckle his dead mother.

Troy spoke with the policeman, who re-holstered his revolver. He moved between the puppies, standing on their backs, and dispatching them with his nightstick, the suckling puppy last. Troy made another call on his mobile and a porter appeared from the hotel with a plastic sack and fire pit tongs – helping the policeman to bag the corpses.

Jessica failed to look away from the scene, transfixed, realising the dogs had as a dignified ending as the lepper on her previous visit to the spice market. Troy walked over. Sumer talked to people in the crowd. Zeynep looked out to sea, past the Chinese Fishing Nets.

'Hey. A bit of excitement, Indian style.' Troy rolled his eyes at Jessica. 'Rabies.'

'Yes, I guessed. And the combined Canadian special forces needed to be involved?'

'Some bloody hic blasting dogs with a gun and playing whack-a-pup just yards from the boss, spreading around virus, is less than ideal. And not in the risk assessment, if I so recall.'

Zeynep casually offered Troy a swig of beer from her bottle. Jessica smiled between the two, more the act of an old married couple than work colleagues.

'To be honest, most of the time I'm just babysitting. A crossing guard – you know? Like your Popsicle Ladies.'

Jessica laughed. 'Lollipop Ladies you mean, who help school kids cross busy roads? You'd be no good as a Lollipop Lady – you would be too scared of our roundabouts!'

'The clever ones are the bosses and their senior staff, like Zeynep here. How they manage to concentrate on their jobs as well as following all these protocols and procedures, is way beyond me.'

Zeynep beamed at her colleague, proud to have been referred to as clever and as *senior staff*; pretending to accept the comment as a simple statement of fact. Troy continued to scan the waterfront and narrow beach, with the occasional glance towards the Canadian family – now back enjoying their late picnic on the balcony, Nadir's back clearly visible against the balustrade, napping.

'Anyway. Back on my head.' Troy stood from his perch on the jetty, stretching.

'Yep, and me.' Zeynep extended a hand for Troy to pull her up.

Sumer sat on a wooden sleeper, fixed along the edge of the jetty. Jessica jumped to her feet and bought two more cold beers from a street vendor. Handing one to Sumer, she sat directly onto the jetty planks, between his legs, to watch the fishermen operate the huge Chinese Fishing Nets, and the seagoing ferries steam through the narrow strait. She leant back against his leg, feeling the bulge in his jeans harden. She snorted a laugh.

'Men!'

*

Jessica went through her usual bedtime routine, this time wearing pyjamas and locking open the catch on the balcony door. She took a beer to the balustrade. Light spilled from the children's window. Diaz's voice, reading a bedtime story, drifted on the land breeze. Jessica watched Troy and Zeynep walk around the pool. They stood still as Zeynep produced a document from her pool bag and handed it to Troy. He carefully scrutinised the text before raising his head to stare at Zeynep. Grabbing her waist, he spun her around as she squealed at him. She smacked his chest, playfully pushing him away. Her body language suggested she was not scared of Troy, but she obviously did not want him manhandling her. Jessica knew that feeling.

Jessica lay back on the bed, she would text or call Jason, before sleep. She closed her eyes for a moment.

'Jess. Jessica. You awake? Sorry.'

'Zeynep!' Jessica stretched and slipped onto the wooden floor, double checking she really wore pyjamas. 'How'd you get in?' Both women looked towards the open balcony door.

'What have you got in your pool bag?'

Zeynep grinned, clutching the bag to her chest.

'I might let you see tomorrow.' She teased.

Jessica growled her response.

'Open the fucking bag, Zeynep, or I scream for the guard. *Simdi!*'

'Jess, please! It is just a letter. That is not why I am here.'

Shakily, Zeynep unzipped her bag and held it open to Jessica. Inside were a few plastic bath toys, junior sunblock, children's beach shoes, and a brown A4 envelope. Jessica cautiously removed the envelope, clearing her view to the bottom of the bag.

'Shit, Zeynep. I am so sorry.' She held out the envelope, making Zeynep flinch. I must have been dreaming again. You shouldn't have just walked in.'

Jessica cautiously opened the desk drawer and peered inside, before slumping into the chair, her face, chest and back running with sweat.

'Jess, I am so sorry. What have I done to you? I should have waited until the morning. I am just a bit excited. I feel so stupid now.'

Jessica saw her friend's eyes well. She jumped to her feet as Zeynep flinched and recoiled. Jessica gathered her into a hug; both women laughed.

'You are not stupid! You are clever and lovely. Just ask Troy. Please don't cry, I feel rotten now! Come on, what's your good news?'

Jessica guided Zeynep to the bed, they sat on the white Egyptian cotton bedspread, crossed legged and facing each other.

'I don't suppose you will now, but I was going to ask if you can have a couple of days off work and come on an adventure.'

'You shouldn't have asked me that, Zeynep! An adventure? Now I will have to say yes!'

'The bosses were due to spend a couple of days cruising the Kerala Backwaters in a converted rice barge.' Zeynep fidgeted with excitement.

'Sure, like you do.'

'Something has come up with the missus and they can't go. She has a couple of meetings, but they can cope alone with the littlies. Some private family time, except for Troy and half the Indian Army. She asked if I want to take the cruise. How exciting? They don't want me to go on my own and I'd love you to come, please.'

Jessica lay back on the bed, running through the working week ahead, in her mind.

'Don't suppose they have wifi?'

'No, but a good 4G mobile signal along most of the river.'

Jessica reached for her iPhone and dialled a contact on speaker phone.

'Hey!'

'Hey Jess! I am in bed, thinking about you. I knew you were thinking of me!'

Jessica turned off the speaker, brought the phone to her ear, cleared her throat and blushed scarlet.

'Mrs Taylor here Sumer, good evening.'

'Sorry Mrs Taylor, I thought ...'

'Something *else* has ... come up,' she could not help but smirk at her own inuendo, 'and I was wondering if you might take things in hand for a couple of days, you know, instead of me keeping ... things in hand. I will be available by mobile and will keep in touch by email. To be honest, I think we both know ...' She let the sentence die. They spoke about a few work items and Jessica rang off.

'Sounded promising, Jess. You are coming? You can invite your friend if you like – they are big boats.'

'My friend? God no. He's more a colleague than a friend. Sumer? God no.'

Zeynep laughed. 'The lady doth protest too much. I meant the friend who visits you. Honestly, it is up to you, just offering.'

'Lideri? I don't think so.' Jessica scoffed.

'I heard you giggling away the other day and I heard you speak Turkish to her.'

'Nah, but thanks. Just not her thing. It would be nice for you to chat with a fellow Turk, but she is a little odd, in many ways. Anyway, it literally couldn't happen.'

'Just us then?'

'Yes, please Zeynep. That will be lovely, lovely, lovely. And I am still intrigued to hear your other news.'

Chapter Six

The captain showed his two guests around the converted rice barge. The hull was traditional coconut fibre coir rope tied jackwood planks, waterproofed with boiled cashew nutshell resin, with a superstructure of bamboo and plaited palm leaves.

'Ok ladies. I have a challenge for you. There is not a single nail or screw used to make your traditional luxury home on the water. I will give you £100 for every nail you can find, and you must pay me £100 for every nail you cannot find!'

Laughing at his own joke, he continued to show them the two ensuite bedrooms, one with mosquito nets open to the forward-looking bow, with a double bed, and one with air-conditioning and super-king-sized bed. The small open galley and wheelhouse stood aft. The deckhand waved enthusiastically from behind the ship's wheel, the cook opened his larder and small refrigerator to reveal a wonderful supply of fresh fruit, vegetables, fish, meat, and rice.

'Ladies, I can sit with you for your three days and two nights, pointing out every bird, animal, and building on your amazing adventure through the brackish lagoons, lakes and rivers of the Kerala Backwaters – following a similar route to my ship's predecessors, laden with the best rice on the planet. Or my crew and I can disappear back into the very jackwood planks, which provide the platform for your journey. But I recommend my bespoke service, designed especially for you two lovely ladies. I will let you relax and watch beautiful Kerala drift past you like a dream. If you need any explanation of the sights, if you want cocktails or to graze on the kitchen between meals, or you want to help sail the boat – please just call my name. My crew and I are here only to make you happy.'

With a flourish, he bowed, smiled, and disappeared to the stern, as the barge gently chugged into the open backwaters. The women decided to both sleep in the air-conditioned cabin and to lift all the palm leaf weaved shutters in the forward cabin – using it as an extension to the deck, a daybed and refuge from the intense sun. They pulled one low wooden sun lounger back into the dappled shade before the deckhand burst into view to move the second lounger and apologise for not having better pre-empted their needs.

Jessica slipped into her bikini bottoms and reclined back onto her lounger with her work's laptop, to check Sumer's weekly production and productivity reports. Zeynep eventually joined her wearing a striking one-piece red costume. Jessica wolf-whistled, making her turn slowly around, complimenting her curves at every angle. Zeynep flopped onto the neighbouring lounger, blushing and giggling as the captain returned with a cocktail, brimming with fruit and vegetables, in a mock goldfish bowl with two straws.

'Work?'

'Just checking-in with Sumer. He really is a gem, but only young; I don't want to leave him unsupervised.'

'Quite a handsome boy.'

Jessica shrugged. Zeynep took a long draft of cocktail, pinching the bridge of her nose with the cold and alcohol rush.

'You two …?'

'Zeynep! I am a married woman.'

Zeynep used her straw to dunk a piece of mango under the liquor.

'We are all very focused on security.' Zeynep mumbled into the cocktail bowl, taking another long suck on the straw. 'I really should not be sitting in the sun, slurping alcohol, and gossiping. I could lose my job, very easily.'

Jessica slid her laptop to one side, remaining quiet to allow her companion to decide if to speak of what worried her. An easy silence passed, Zeynep engrossed with her thoughts.

'You brought Sumer into the hotel.'

'For afternoon tea following a busy Saturday morning at work. And?'

'Will you bring him into the hotel again, whilst we are here?'

'Sweetheart, we are going to have a brilliant few days together; I am so glad you invited me. But who I bring into the hotel is nothing to do with … anyone. How do you even know he came in for tea? And why does anyone care?'

'Troy saw you with him at the charity autorickshaw parade. He asked me and I agreed that there could be something going on between you. Troy doesn't miss a trick, he checked with reception. The receptionist had seen Sumer's name written on a gift you gave him.'

'Right. This conversation is over Zeynep, let us not fall out. There is nothing going on, it is nobody's business except Sumer's and mine, plus he is a sweet, gentle guy, who poses no security risk, to anyone. And if I do want to shag my colleague, I won't be asking Troy's permission, or yours.'

Jessica lay back on the lounger, closing her eyes.

'May I tell you something about sweet, gentle Sumer, Jess?' Jessica did not respond. 'Sumer is a Brahmin. A high caste. Do you know this, Jess?' Jessica sniffed and cleared her throat but did not respond further. 'His family owns huge tracts of farmland, some with poor tenant farmers. Their empire stretches to grain silos, warehouses, distribution networks, logistic companies, import and export corporations. Some years they lend money to the bank – I don't mean they have savings; I mean they set interest rates and the bank borrows money from them.'

'Look, this is ridiculous. Troy has gone to all this effort to spy on a random friend that I slept with once, just because I am staying in a room near your boss. Not that I am saying I did actually sleep with him, or anything. I am really uncomfortable having this conversation, behind my husband's back.'

'Sumer's family and associates were known to Troy, long before he was *known* to you Jess. He has extended family in all areas of public and professional life. Engineers like himself, politicians, priests, business, military, teachers.'

'And you are holding having a hardworking family, against him?'

'He asked to move from Chennai to help you in the new office, following a series of corruption allegations and the suspicious suicides of two prominent protesting farmers. Farmers protesting at Sumer's family's corporate monopoly over domestic and export markets, and government legislation which will strengthen their stranglehold over them. Protesting farmers who are very publicly supported and championed by my boss and the Canadian government, against the best interests of Sumer and his associates.'

'Are you saying Sumer is a murderer and a, I don't know, mafia don or terrorist?' Jessica went to drink cocktail through her sparkly straw – but Zeynep had already drained the two-litre bowl.

'For our sake, I am asking you say nothing to him about our stay. Say nothing. We were due to checkout of Branston today for this trip and then back ... well, onwards. But we will be gone soon. And, as your friend, I hope you will seriously consider your continued relationship with him.'

'We have no fucking *relationship*!'

*

With a belly full of cocktail and the sun high in the sky, Zeynep fell almost immediately to sleep as she lay back on her lounger, next to Jessica. They were becoming close friends, despite bickering over Sumer. Zeynep rested a hand on Jessica's lounger, tucking her middle finger into the waist of Jessica's tiny bikini bottoms. Jessica reciprocated, gently holding Zeynep's wrist, as she lightly snored.

Jessica had no reason to gossip about the Canadians with Sumer. She would honour her friend's request, even though she was certain he posed no threat. They had not spoken about why he had requested the transfer from Chennai, Jessica assumed he was just *stepping-up* and developing his career. Neither had they spoken about family – it would have felt disloyal to talk about Jason, and she had no interest in meeting his mother. But judging from the stifling, tiny bedroom, with squeaking bedstead and lumpy mattress – he was not being supported by a successful industrialist or crime family.

Zeynep woke to the sound of singing schoolgirls on the towpath. The barge slowly steamed just feet from the edge. Jessica had already jumped up and was tying a silk throw around her bare chest, waving to the girls, and joining in the song. The girls were all dressed in blue and white school uniform – some in pleated skirts, some in saris, and the remainder in shalwar kameez and hijab, depending on their religion or sponsoring church. The girls ran along the path, swirling, dipping and dancing in perfect time, to an obviously well-rehearsed routine. Jessica knew the dance steps. Mirroring the girls as she sung, she danced along the boat's gunnels, towards the stern. As the boat left the girls behind, they gathered in a loose group waving, as they and Jessica both gave each other an encore. Jessica returned to Zeynep with two beers from the galley – insisting she be allowed to carry them herself.

Jessica sat on Zeynep's bed, slipping out of the throw, and snuggled up to her. There was no way that either woman would have allowed a bad atmosphere to develop between them.

'Just so you know Zeynep, I am not planning to mention you all to anyone. I won't even mention you to Jason, until after you have gone.' Zeynep grinned, dipping her head to nudge Jessica, in reply.

The two women watched a man dive under the water to retrieve whelks, dropping them into a floating pot. Another dived for fine sand, which he unloaded from a pail into a dugout canoe and would sell on to a builder's merchant.

'And you have some good news to tell me. Or had you forgotten?'

'Forgotten? No way. I had to tell Diaz and Cameron before I could tell you. You are the fourth person, plus me, in the whole world to know! Well, I whispered it to the sleeping children, but that doesn't really count. I was going to sneak back to yours after I had told the others – but I heard you chatting to your friend. She visits at strange times.' She made eye contact with Jessica, waiting for an explanation. Jessica expected another security lecture, but Zeynep eventually continued. 'Are you ready? No, actually I will show you.'

Zeynep retrieved her gadget bag from hidden under the daybed and tumbled the combination lock. She brought out the brown envelope bearing a consulate stamp.

'Go on, have a peek.' Jessica pulled out another sealed envelope. 'Oops! Sorry Jess, I didn't realise that was there. Have another look.'

Jessica handed the sealed envelope to Zeynep and pulled out an impressive certificate, from the original envelope, in French and English – complete with crest and maple leaf. A photo identity card fell to the lounger. Jessica studied the certificate.

'Your Canadian citizenship! Oh my God Zeynep, congratulations.'

Jessica leant to hug her friend as the excitement became too much for Zeynep to contain. She dragged Jessica to her feet and clamped her to her chest. With both woman laughing and squealing, they jumped around in a circle, Jessica concentrating hard on protecting the certificate from damage. The captain appeared, smiling at the commotion, and confirmed he had a bottle of champagne for just such an emergency.

*

The two women enjoyed an impressive supper together. The cook arranged the table on the deck, with flowers and candles. Both women wore cocktail dresses. Zeynep wore a zebra striped body-hugging dress, slashed provocatively to reveal strips of flesh from just under her breasts, to just above the short hem; there was nowhere to hide underwear. Jessica wore an old favourite; a short, low, silk designer dress with a moody blue and deep red print – designed to resemble a sexy nightdress. She had bought it, before marrying Jason, to impress a previous lover, but it was exceptional quality and lasted well.

The two eventually retired, late. They both lay on their backs, exposing themselves to the cooling, dehumidifying air-conditioning, holding hands from across the expanse of the super-king-sized-bed.

'What will your parents think about the Canadian citizenship? They won't worry you might forget them?'

'My mum died when I was young. So did my brother.'

'Oh Zeynep, that is awful. I am sorry.' Jessica sat up onto her elbows, using the silk throw to cover her naked body. 'Would you like my mother? You can have her. No really.'

Zeynep laughed. 'You are so funny Jess. I think that is why I love you.'

Jessica lay back against Zeynep's shoulder, bringing Zeynep's arm to drape around her neck.

'That is what Lideri says. Father? Dare I ask?'

'I actually don't really know my father. A real scandal in rural Turkey, twenty odd years ago. My mum eventually married her childhood sweetheart – such a brave and decent thing for him to do, as mum already had me. I kind of stuck out a bit – being mixed-race. But my stepdad also died, and I ended up living with his bachelor brother. Again, very kind of him to take me in, but got the tongues wagging. An old man moving-in a young girl, who wasn't even blood related. This citizenship will secure my future. Whatever happens with the Andersons, I will never have to go back picking tea, or find myself some old husband.'

'Troy is a lot older than you. Must be twice your age. I have seen you two together; he only has eyes for you.'

Zeynep scoffed. 'Absolutely not Jess. Never in a million years.'

'He might not think that. You melted in his arms when he swung you around last night.'

Zeynep laughed. 'I don't think so Jess.'

'Is being a Canadian's au pair enough to gain citizenship?'

'No, not exactly. But Troy and Cameron definitely helped. Diaz has always fought my corner, ever since bringing me into her scheme. We really are like a family, the six of us. Troy and Cameron go way back.'

'Provost together?'

'Yes, military.'

'Scheme for orphans?'

'Kind of. Strange you should say that. I think of myself as abandoned by my father, not orphaned. I guess he is still breathing, somewhere.'

'How did your mum meet a foreigner, coming from a Turkish village?'

Zeynep slid around on the bed until their faces met, upside down. She kissed the tip of Jessica's nose, 'Nosey!' before kissing her firmly on the lips, with mouth clamped shut. A command for silence, rather than with any sapphic spark.

*

The women settled into an easy routine the following day. Zeynep seldom drank alcohol when working or when around the Andersons; neither did she have many children-uninterrupted sleeps. On her backwaters adventure, she did plenty of both.

Jessica was more active. She helped steer the boat; the captain trusting her to take it through some of the narrower waterways. She cooked lunch - a Mandarin Chicken Sauté over a bed of steaming Indian rice with sultanas and roasted cashew nuts, for both her friend and the crew. She also started her exit strategy proposal, for Company management. She used reports and information from Sumer and mapped out which responsibilities she would take away to Portsmouth, which Sumer could take over, and what needed the overview of a manager based in Kochi or Chennai.

Feeling a little squiffy following a large glass of pinot in the afternoon, she wore her skimpiest bikini to video call Sumer – watching his eyes move around his computer screen. Titillated by the attention, she then took her top off completely to video call Jason, knowing he would be sat in his office at the end of a long shift. She walked him around the barge, purposely introducing the crew, still topless, to tease her husband further. They arranged a Teams date night for the following Friday.

Calling for another large glass of pinot, she settled down on her lounger in the shade of the plaited palm leaf canopy, the laptop propped on a low table.

'You look so cute, when you are tipsy, Bambi. Your cheeks and the very tip of your nose glows red, your eyes sparkle, and you have a permanent smirk.'

'What does your friend Priti look like when she is tipsy?'

'I am not sure. Next time I'll leave the bedside lamp on, so I can see properly.'

The cheeky response was a high-risk strategy, especially as Jessica had been drinking. Her eyes narrowed for a moment, before her cheekbones raised with a wide grin. She scoffed.

'Touché. So, I had a regular Buddha moment on Sunday. I walked through the spice quarter of Fort Kochi. I saw a new life being conceived. A young life starting on a generational journey through perpetual poverty – never to be free because of her caste. And a lepper at the end of life, slumped dead in the gutter. I'm atheist as you know, but I can understand why both great and simple minds strive to make sense of life's little challenges. And my God, India is a widescreen, full-HD, cinematic view of humanity – no wonder Bollywood is the largest film industry on the planet. On any one day you can hear mothers giving birth behind the thin walls of a shack, see people defecating at the side of the road, or whole families bathing naked in a stream or under a public standpipe. And all that in relatively prosperous Kerala. I have made a good friend at work, from a high caste, privileged, wealthy family. Whilst in Kochi, even they are staying in a poky, humid hostel with a squeaky … um, you know, like a squeaky … ceiling fan.'

'Deep, man.'

'Yeah. My other news is – I'm starting a plan to come home. Not long now. If you still want me home.'

'Hey! Don't even say that jokingly. Of course I want you home, I never wanted you to leave in the first place. And I am certainly missing you. All of you!'

His two fingers loomed towards the camera, before diverting towards the screen, Jessica knew where he was pointing.

'No!' She squealed with a grin, covering her breasts with her hands. 'Wait until Friday, cheeky.'

'Um, move your hands young lady, I can't see them!'

With her best sexy pout, Jessica removed one hand from her breast, slipped a finger fully into her mouth and, with the moistened finger, ended the call.

*

'Do you and *never-in-a-million-years*-Troy talk about everything?'

'We are close. Like I said, one big family. After the horror of my conception and early life that followed …'

Zeynep blushed deeply and looked out the window of the Ambassador Taxi, bumping along the dirt track towards the metalled highway and the hotel.

'But Troy is always guarded. By nurture and by nature. Are you still annoyed at his distrust of the boy, Sumer?'

Jessica grinned and playfully slapped her arm. The two locked fingers, like sisters on a family jaunt from the beach.

'He is a man, not a boy. That much I do know! He must be at least your age. But no, has Troy ever mentioned Mr Singh the concierge? Troy was all but bullying Mr Singh on Monday morning. And the police were there.'

'Nothing to worry about. Troy wanted him to hand-in his old pistol while we are there.'

'And he couldn't just ask the hotel manager to have a word? I mean, Mr Singh is a lovely old guy – the police, really?'

'Ah yes, sweet, gentle, Mr Gurdit Singh. Wandering around with his loaded ornate firearm and his decorative bludgeon.'

'Zeynep!'

'We share a sense of humour, Jessica, and a healthy mistrust of privileged people's children ...' Zeynep fell silent and looked at her lap. Jessica squeezed her hand. 'That was rude and wicked of me. I love those children. They are like my own kids, my own ... baby siblings.' A tear ran down her cheek. She sniffed, cleared her throat, and wiped the back of her free hand across her face. 'You just love everyone Jess, don't you? You love your husband, you *love* your colleague, you love yourself, you love the hotel security guard.' More tears flowed. 'God, I wish I could love another adult.'

Zeynep picked up the now opened envelope, which had been in the High Commission document envelope with her citizenship certificate. She held it up, as if it contained her cynicism, before scrunching it into her blue striped pool bag.

'Phew!' Zeynep let out a long sigh. 'Ok. Gurdit Singh is a 182. Not a direct threat, but a 182'er like many others in his community. You won't see him as a bad person, you will see him as a warrior freedom fighter. The strong brave warrior tribe of *Lions*, of *Singhs*!'

'Hey Zeynep, ease off. You don't know me! I don't even know what a 182 is, let alone support them!'

Zeynep tugged her hand away from Jessica, but she refused to release it.

'And we know you are still in contact with your Kurdish friends!'

'Enough Zeynep. Enough. I don't know what is in your envelope to upset you so much, but it wasn't me who put it there.'

Zeynep continued to pull her hand away, Jessica continued to grip harder, until their knuckles cracked. Zeynep tried again to relax.

'182 refers to the Air India Flight, from Montreal to London on the way to Mumbai, which was blown up over the Atlantic. Mostly Canadians died. You probably don't know about it. 182'ers is Troy's nickname, or code, for any Sikh separatist. Your Mr Gurdit Singh is a separatist and can proudly trace his family lineage along a long line of thorns in Canada's side.'

'I know of Air India Flight 182. It happened weeks after I was born, so I am a bit sketchy on detail. What is in the envelope? Bad news? Problem with the citizenship?'

'I shouldn't say.'

'Zeynep?'

Jessica slid closer to her friend, kissing a tear on her cheek. She licked the corner of a tissue and wiped mascara from under her eyes. Zeynep closed the privacy screen behind the driver. The noise of the overworked petrol engine, and worn suspension knocking over every rut, made it unlikely he would overhear. She tilted her face towards Jessica, their noses almost touching.

'Just DNA results for the babies. Troy asked me to arrange them through the consulate, via labs in Canada. It is another new layer of surveillance, should they ever, God forbid, be kidnapped or worse, and need positively identifying by some foreign law enforcement agency. We have their fingerprints, mug shots and everything. Like they are criminals, instead of innocents.'

The couple stayed in position, resting opposite sides of their faces against the high backrests of the classic, British designed car. Jessica smelt the mint on her friend's breath. Zeynep tilted her head until their foreheads touched.

'I don't know Jess. The report is thorough and anonymous to the lab. It records the full individual codes and confirms, obviously, that the two are siblings. I only share my DNA with one living person that I am aware of, and he took advantage of my mother's love and then abandoned us. Thank God, Jessica, thank God, that a string of unrelated men has looked out for me over the years, and here I am. But I don't *love* them like a father or a brother, and they don't *love* me in that way either. At least I have something in common with my stepfather, uncle, Cameron, and Troy – I also do not know myself well enough – to really *love* me.'

Chapter Seven

Mr Singh met the women as the taxi came to a halt, taking both their bags to the lobby. His welcome sounded sincere, his catchphrase the same, but he looked older and tired, less imposing; the pistol and ebony nightstick missing.

Cameron sat in chinos and a blue university crewneck sweatshirt with two suited businessmen, at the same table where Sumer and Jessica enjoyed their post tryst afternoon tea. Troy stood at the rear entrance to the pool, with good visibility of the pool and a sightline to include Cameron and the front door. The bellboy took the women's bags to leave outside their bedroom doors. Zeynep handed Jessica her remaining pool bag.

'Can you hang onto this please? It has my money and passport. I am just going to see Diaz and the kids. From where Troy is standing, I am guessing she is in the pool.'

Jessica took the pool bag and hugged her friend for a long moment.

'Thanks again Zeynep. That was a lovely trip. I'll thank the Andersons when they are not so busy. Just knock on my door when you want the bag, I am going to freshen-up.'

Zeynep slipped past her working boss but, noticing her, he called her back for a hug. She appeared to tense, before gesturing to Jessica; he waved. Jessica returned the wave and gave a double thumbs-up, referring to the cruise. He brought his hand down to dismiss her thanks. Troy stepped forward with a smile, but Zeynep brushed passed him and out to the pool.

Jessica set the bath running. She had climbed refreshed into the taxi, but the transfer back to the hotel was hot, noisy, dusty, and mentally draining - with Zeynep's mood swings.

She thought about calling Sumer, to check everything was ok in the office. Once she had bathed and changed, it would be too late to meet at work. Perhaps they could meet at his room – she would not expose him to Troy's bullying by inviting him to the hotel. She was not sure if he had a roommate, she would have to ask; it felt like being a teenager again.

Jessica slipped her hand down the front of her linen slacks, thinking first of Sumer, and then Jason.

She had a date night planned, for less than thirty hours away; wondering if she could spend some time with Sumer, but still appear fresh for her husband, on their Teams video date. The bath gurgled as water poured down the overflow. Jessica sprung to her feet to turn off the taps, sending Zeynep's pool bag spilling across the floor.

Returning from the bathroom, she picked up the bag and the spilled envelope, containing the children's DNA results. Distracting herself from the urge to contact Sumer or taking her thoughts of him alone to the bath, she checked the deadlock on the bedroom door and closed the curtains over the balcony windows, before emptying the envelope onto the bed.

Inside were four photographic quality squares of card. Each one had a different reference number ending 021, 022, 023, 024. There were boxes for name, date of birth and sex – each one marked *Anon*. Each card had a barcode style graphic running vertically – representing the subject's unique DNA code, with a corresponding table of numerical codes.

A fifth card was a receipt showing transit and anti-contamination security and control tag numbers. The sixth and final card listed a summary of results, with percentage accuracy. 021 and 022 showed as fully sharing DNA. 023 showed as sharing half of 021 and 022 DNA. 024 showed no relation to the others tested.

*

The couple arranged to meet in Spice Market. Jessica had the kitchen prepare four takeout picnic chicken and seafood salads, with four lidded cups of iced coffees. Her taxi pulled close to the alley entrance where Sumer waited, waving as she walked towards him, smiling. She detoured to the remaining leppers, giving them each a salad and coffee, with a crisp, new 500 rupee note. She offered to shake hands, but neither man complied.

'Sorry to drag you out after work Sumer. I fancied a walk and a quick chat before tomorrow's early team meeting.'

'My pleasure Jess. I would have persuaded my roommate to give us some privacy, he wouldn't have minded.'

Jessica shrugged.

'Another time. I am alone in the hotel next week. Perhaps you could come for tea again. Or, you know, a spot of supper and stuff.'

'Alone? Is our excellency the Canadian High Commissioner to India leaving Kochi?'

'Who?'

Sumer laughed. 'I saw him at the charity autorickshaw parade. I guess the pretty foreign girl is on the team, and the *heavy* with the influential photo ID card?'

Jessica shrugged again.

'Your Canadian cousins are not doing India any favours, at the moment. They are stirring-up trouble with poor, ignorant countryfolk, and trying to keep our agriculture in the dark ages. All the while, their own industrial scale prairie farms are flooding world markets with grain. They should be made an example of.'

'Sorry? How so?'

'For a start, the government should summons and then very publicly expel your hotel friends, back to Canada. Give the agitators something to think about.'

Jessica found a clear section of sandy beach at the end of the spice wharf, spread the large white *Branston* napkins to sit on and handed Sumer his salad. One of the beggars was especially ill and deformed, Jessica had lost her appetite.

Finishing her iced coffee, she lay back on her hands and closed her eyes, realising her short summer dress would rise higher, but she did not adjust it. They lay together in the shadows of a secluded spot. Sumer knew his way around this dress, the same Jessica wore on the day she went to his room. He unzipped the dress and slid his left hand inside her top. She returned his kissing. His right hand slid inside her thigh and to inside her pants. She moved apart her legs, consenting. She then reciprocated contact, slipping a hand inside his trousers.

*

Jessica spent the morning distributing her exit plan and incorporating reviews from more senior managers and suggestions from her own team; Sumer was keen to take on more responsibilities.

Jessica compartmentalised her life as a coping mechanism. Having time away from Jason, to give them both space, was her previous priority – so she volunteered for the India job and threw herself into the project. Now the priority was to move back home, identify her next job with head office, and immerse herself back into her marriage.

She realises how she makes mistakes in life, as much as the next person, and can leave trails of collateral damage. But her priority was to give Jason and herself some space for the good of their marriage. Collecting a lover or two along the way was not ideal, but it was manageable.

The party at the airport hotel and sleeping with the airline pilot on her first full night away was probably unnecessary but huge amounts of fun; he was most proficient. And then hooking up with Sumer had been cathartic – like having a budgerigar to look after. He was sweet, cute, and keen. What he lacked in skill and experience, he made up with youth and enthusiasm.

Jessica took another malaria tablet. She had forgotten to take the medication on her trip to the Kerala Backwaters, and so took Thursday evening's dose as usual, an extra tablet Friday morning and an extra tablet Friday lunchtime. She took her Friday evening dose as soon as she returned from work – to ensure she did not forget it on date night with Jason.

Mr Singh greeted her. Without asking for consent, she gave him a long hug. He did not bother checking to see if hotel management noticed.

'Time to pour me a tea, Mr Singh?'

They sat together, outside his security lodge.

'Thank you for the hug, Mrs Taylor. I am wondering if there is a reason.'

'Only that you are a lovely man, and you are looking down in the mouth. Our Commonwealth cousins still making trouble for you?'

'They don't occupy my homeland, but they are not especially helpful either.' Jessica raised an eyebrow, for him to continue. 'Your friend Mr Troy had the police run some checks – the hotel is not pleased. But my day brightens when I see my lovely guests looking happy. How many times did you have to smile at your husband before he married you? Twice? Once?' Jessica giggled and flashed him a bashful smile. 'I will be honest with you Mrs Taylor. A few years younger and they may have had good cause to fear me. They even made me swap my father's Kirpan, which I have worn since I was younger than you, for a blunt, decorative knife. Humiliating.' He pulled aside his traditional military style tunic to reveal a brass handled decorative Kirpan in a blue leather sheath. It looked like a child's toy. 'Sometimes Mrs Taylor, size is important.'

'Chin-up! Troy won't be here forever.'

She kissed his forehead and headed for the lobby before he could stand to escort her. Tomorrow, she would write a personal email to the hotel manager, praising Mr Singh for his hard work, safe hands, and support during her nightmare hallucination. She would also find a reason to kick Troy in the shin again. Troy may stare down this lion-of-a-man, a born warrior – but he was no match for her.

*

Jessica planned to video call Jason as they both soaked in the bath, as part of date night. But that did not stop her having a long soak in preparation. She shaved, plucked, trimmed, and waxed, using an expensive moisturiser to ensure all the areas, which Jason would concentrate on, looked their best.

She skipped around the room to her Spotify playlist, moving occasional tables and stools around – so she could move seamlessly between venues, maintaining the optimum camera angles. She would tap *connect*, on her Teams video conference app and then run onto the shared balcony, wearing just knickers and her silk throw. She would then slink towards the camera, blowing Jason a kiss, moving to the sofa for a catchup. Then she would strip naked in front of Jason, moving to the already drawn bath – complete with candles, floating candles and rose petals on top of the bubbles. She placed a folded towel on the nightstand in preparation, to rest her laptop. When room service arrived, she would hold the smallest towel around her chest. She would spin the camera around, so Jason could see her walk to the door, still dripping bathwater, towel gaping open at the back. She had coasters piled one end of the desk to angle the laptop, so they could eat together – her both topless, and perfectly framed. She would *accidentally* spill yoghurt over her breasts, to scoop it into her mouth with her finger – whilst maintaining eye contact. Eventually she would take her laptop, and therefore her husband, to bed, propping it on the bedside cabinet. She checked the camera angle several times, knowing exactly which way to lie. They would make virtual love; she would call out his name. They would fall asleep together. In the morning, she would blow a kiss and wave, before disconnecting. Her Indian exit/marital kickstart plan in motion.

The door knocked. She looked through the peephole to see Troy standing outside, head turning to scan the corridor. He would hear her music and see the light through the peephole change, as she brought her eye close. But she ignored him anyway – he was a dick and she did not have the inclination to be his audience tonight. Whatever he wanted, it would wait until tomorrow.

She returned to her laptop and tapped *connect*. She wore Jason's favourite pants, having bought them in a pack of three from Victoria Secret for work; she did not think them especially sexy. She checked out her bottom in the mirror, as Teams conferencing rang Jason's laptop. Perhaps they were quite flattering. Black see-through with frilly white piping, they narrowed at the back, accentuating the roundness of her buttocks.

Shit! I wore these with Sumer!

She did not want to cancel the connection and snub her husband even for a moment, but neither could she wear the same underwear which another man had touched and enjoyed. She tugged them down just as Jason appeared on the screen. Trying to kick them off and stand to her full height, composing her sexy pout and seductively licking her lips, she fell backwards with a scream. Jason saw her legs fly into the air, the pants wrapped around both ankles, and heard her bottom thud against the floorboards. Her head snapped backwards hitting the soft edge of the sofa.

'Um. Jess, are you ok?'

Through the moaning about her sore bottom and hip, Jessica began laughing, a full belly laugh. As always, Jason had to join in. She managed to sit up and bring the camera to her face but could not speak and barely managed to breathe through the laughter. The opening scene of her *exit-from-India-date-night* could not have gone better, if she had planned it.

*

Everything else went to plan; Jason so infatuated, he could think of nothing of himself to talk about. After their long-distance lovemaking, she lay back on top of the thin, white duvet, purring and moaning – keeping herself fully exposed to the camera and Jason, six-thousand miles away.

They whispered to each other about the great times they had already shared and those yet to come. Jessica knew more work was required to pull their marriage back on track, but at least she had taken the first crucial steps. She was ready; *she could do this.*

Chapter Eight

All but one of the candles burnt out. The footsteps and shadow outside Jessica's balcony window, brought her to a sitting position.

'Mr Singh? Is that you out there?'

'Jess? Who is there?'

'Jason! You startled me. There is someone on the balcony, I will check. It is not a problem, either Mr Singh the concierge, or one of the soldiers.'

'No Jess! Don't you check. Phone down to reception, and why are there soldiers in the hotel?'

'Stop fussing and relax. I might want you to talk dirty to me in a minute.' She wrinkled her nose into a smile.

Jessica opened her balcony and peered right, towards the landing entrance. She saw a figure, perhaps Singh holding his ebony nightstick. They looked at each other in the near darkness. The figure raised a hand. Jessica waved back and nodded, returning inside and double checking the balcony door was secure.

She sat on the sofa and took a swig of water from the half empty tumbler sat on the desk, next to the remains of her curry. Her head spun. She had been in the middle of a complicated dream. The plot of the dream was already lost to her, but she knew Zeynep and Lideri were arguing in Turkish. Lideri was jealous about something.

She closed her eyes, composing herself, before planning on returning to Jason on the Teams video. The plot of the dream drifted into her consciousness, like a short-term memory. She half-heard the heavy mortice lock and bolt thrown on the connecting door.

Two gunshots rang out, sounding close; for a moment, she thought they may have come from inside her own bedroom. All of the candles were now extinguished, she must have slept again sitting up, the room now lit only by the laptop screen and the swimming pool lights shining around the closed voile curtains. She ran to the bedroom door, locking the heavy old mortice with the brass key, slipping the night latch deadlock button. She checked the heavy brass bolt on the connecting door and hid by the side of the bed, away from the balcony window.

Shouting and banging began outside her room. Jason called her name, she whispered for him to stay quiet. The shouting continued outside, followed by a rhythmic thudding against a nearby door. She buried her face in her hands and placed two fingers in her ears. Lideri had once sang to Jessica when they were trapped in a tunnel in Turkey. Months afterwards, Lideri taught her the song, they found it on You Tube – Jessica now sung it quietly to herself.

*

Jessica barely finished singing the first verse when she heard a glass window smash, followed by a woman screaming the children's names.

'Sorry Jason, I can't stay out of this.'

Jason shouted as Jessica closed the laptop lid, to silence him. Through her peephole in the bedroom door, she saw

Diaz restrained by an Indian soldier and the backs of two other soldiers breaking into Zeynep and the children's room. She slipped the locks and walked barefoot into the corridor, pulling her short summer dressing gown around her naked body. The restraining soldier glared at her, but she continued to Diaz, embracing the woman as she screamed. The soldiers were now inside the children's room.

'Put your guns down! Put your fucking guns down, my children are in that room!'

One soldier returned to the door, shrugged, and wobbled his head towards the restraining soldier, turning back to continue searching the room. Soldiers and hotel staff, with first aid equipment and white towels from the housekeeper's trolley, piled into the Anderson's room next door. Jessica stood inside the children's room, almost identical to her own, but with an additional narrow bed against the wall. Zeynep's room had two connecting doors, as opposed to Jessica's one.

The desk drawer drew her attention. She pointed and a bemused soldier opened the drawer to reveal the complimentary books, including a similar hardback copy of Salman Rushdie's Midnight's Children. She scanned the room again, knelt and carefully slid open the oversized blanket drawer from under the fourposter bed.

'Hey sweetie. It's all ok, you are safe. There is lots going on, but it's all cool. Let's go and find Diaz, she is worried about all three of you.'

Zeynep clutched the two sleeping children, her breathing laboured, panting through gritted teeth, spittle around her nose and mouth. The soldiers moved towards the bed, but Jessica raised a restraining hand. Slowly she helped Zeynep from the drawer, both children still clamped to her chest. She led her towards the open door and Diaz, who now thrashed to be released from the restraining soldier. The children hung like ragdolls from her arms – obviously breathing but in a seemingly uncomfortable, even painful clench.

As the four reached the door, Jessica saw the brass handle of a knife, clenched in Zeynep's hand. In that split second, she imagined it might be Singh's Kirpan. She closed her own hand around Zeynep's.

'Darling. I need you to put down the children, Diaz will keep them safe. *Simdi, Zeynep, simdi. Lutfen.*' Zeynep met Jessica's eye and nodded. 'There are men here with guns. I also need you to give me the knife, without making a fuss.'

The soldiers both snapped their assault rifles to their shoulders and aimed at the four. Jessica shifted position to block their aim on Zeynep. Diaz screamed at the soldiers to lower their guns. Still gripping Zeynep's hand into a fist containing the knife, she placed her free hand behind Zeynep's neck, forcing her to look Jessica fully in the face.

'Good girl. Now, let the children slip to the floor.'

Jessica nodded as she spoke and Zeynep mirrored her nodding. She bent at the waist, lowering the children. Once most of their bodies lay on the floorboards, she finally released her grip. Gregory's head banged against the floor; Nadia flopped on top of him, neither stirred from their sleep. She gripped the knife harder. Jessica made the split-second decision to move Zeynep, with the knife, away from the children – both protecting the children and reducing the chance of the soldiers shooting Zeynep.

Jessica punched Zeynep in the chest with the heels of both hands, sending her sprawling backwards onto the floor. She stepped over the children towards Zeynep – creating a shield between Zeynep and the children, and Zeynep and the soldiers. Diaz broke free and grabbed both children from the floor, a soldier moved to reach Zeynep, but tripped over Diaz. His assault rifle discharged a single shot into the heavy stone wall, causing plaster and stone to plume out across the corridor. Zeynep skidded and scrambled backwards into the Anderson's open door, Jessica in pursuit.

Several soldiers, whose sole instruction was to protect the High Commissioner first, and his immediate family second, aimed their assault rifles at Jessica and Zeynep. They did not shout warnings or instructions, they simply aimed, ready to kill. Cameron lay on a blood-soaked bed, a soldier and two hotel staff stemming the flow of pumping blood with towel compressions. Troy lay on the floor in the centre of his own scarlet aura, emanating from a wound to his chest. No one attended to him, he was obviously dead.

Zeynep straddled Troy's chest and shouted '*No!*' into his face.

'Jessica! They have killed him. They will kill the children!'

The soldiers circled Zeynep, keeping out of each other's line of fire. Jessica moved closer, trying to protect her friend. Closer than the soldiers, she was the first to see Zeynep reach for Troy's pistol, clutched in his lifeless hand. To protect herself from Zeynep, and Zeynep from the soldiers, Jessica kicked her under the chin. The pistol discharged into the ceiling and flew from Zeynep's hand across the room.

Jessica slipped in Troy's blood and fell heavily onto her back. Zeynep made it to the connecting door, helplessly tugging and pushing against the handle. A soldier brought the butt of his rifle hard between her shoulder blades.

Jessica lay winded on the floor; head to one side, her cheek in the pool of Troy's blood. She focused on Mr Singh, spreadeagled on the floor; a soldier held a bayonetted rifle firmly to the back of his neck.

Chapter Nine

'Mrs Taylor, we appreciate your assistance.'

Jessica studied the two detectives. A uniform stood by the door. The male who spoke had a kind, studious, bespectacled face. His colleague female, with the beautiful eyes of many women Jessica saw around Fort Kochi – a mix of Indian and Portuguese heritage. Her expression stern. Jessica had seen them previously, talking with Mr Singh in the courtyard.

'My pleasure.' Jessica held up her handcuffed wrists. 'Where am I?'

'You are in hospital, Mrs Taylor. I am Detective Mahatma; this is Detective Indira.'

'Hospital? Really? I think I had guessed that much!'

'You are safe in a military hospital. We have reason not to tell you the exact location, but we will of course drop you back to your hotel, or another if you prefer, presently.'

'Why? Are the Anderson's here?' She held up the handcuffs again.

The male smiled, inclining his head. The female spoke.

'We were advised that you can be quite … quite aggressive. Best to keep us all safe, Mrs Taylor.'

Jessica scoffed.

'Where is Mr Singh?'

Indira spoke again.

'Mrs Taylor. You remain a person of interest to us, nothing more ...'

'A person of interest? Me? You are joking! If it wasn't for me, your soldiers would have shot Zeynep and probably one or both children! Me, *a person of interest*?'

'Your dressing gown is covered in a murder victim's blood and gunfire residue ...'

'Because a gun was fired whilst I was slipping in his pool of blood. Just ask your soldier friends – have they bodycams?'

Mahatma removed his round wire spectacles and polished them on the lining of his brown linen suit jacket.

'Let us start by having a detailed timeline for your evening Mrs Taylor.'

Jessica explained why she left the office early, for her prearranged date night. Mahatma raised an eyebrow, failing to understand why a catchup with her husband required two baths and rearranging furniture around her room. Indira slid her hand discretely on the tabletop to silence her senior colleague – she would explain later. Jessica did not detail exactly what action led her husband and herself to fall asleep together but blushed deeply as Indira established durations and times for each of the date night events.

'You have no witnesses to this ... date night?'

'No! Obviously. Well, not exactly. My husband, of course, in full Technicolor. Also, room service. And Troy knocked on my door. And I saw Mr Singh later in the evening, just before … Or perhaps not Mr Singh, perhaps a soldier. It was dark.'

'We will come back to each alibi again, Mrs Taylor. But first, did Troy come into your room?'

'*Again*? *Alibi*? This isn't a chat; it is an interrogation! No, I ignored him. Perhaps he went on to his muse's room – Zeynep. Why are you quizzing me?'

Kindly Mahatma inclined his head in sympathy and took over the questioning from his colleague.

'We really do sympathise Mrs Taylor. This has been awful for you. And I am inclined to agree – you did your best to protect an anxious au pair and the innocent children. But we want to ask about your other visitors, please.

'Your lover Sumer texted and came to the hotel to see you?'

Indira slid over a CCTV printout of Sumer stood at the hotel reception and another of him walking towards the table, at which they previously enjoyed their afternoon tea.

'Look, I don't know where you got the whole *lover* thing from …'

Mahatma smiled. 'Sumer is in our custody, Mrs Taylor. Perhaps he is lying? I wonder why else he might have come to the hotel just before the High Commissioner is assassinated. Such a mystery.'

'Assassinated? Oh my God, is Cameron dead? Poor Diaz. Poor children.'

Indira flicked a look of disappointment to her colleague. He sheepishly polished his glasses again.

'Shit! Look, yes. We were briefly lovers. I am trying to save my marriage. I ... Look, Sumer is a lovely kid.'

'But you saw him?'

'No!'

'He texted you from the lobby, asking to meet.' Indira held an evidence bag containing Jessica's iPhone.

'No. I did not see any text. I was, I had my mind elsewhere. You must see that I did not respond to any text during my date with Jason.'

'And the visit from your other *friend*? Or is that *other lover?*'

'Who? Troy or Mr Singh? Absolutely not! No way!'

Indira maintained eye contact. Mahatma referred to his open notebook.

'Lideri?'

'Lideri! We are not lovers, God no. I didn't see Lideri last night, I was having a lovely day. She only visits when I am feeling down, to comfort me, I guess. To make me laugh ...' Jessica tailed off. 'She isn't a friend in the *normal* sense. Look, just check the CCTV footage; I can assure you, you will not see her.'

'You were heard arguing, in Turkish. We need her contact details.'

'No! That is impossible. Who said it was in Turkish? Who else speaks Turkish around here, to recognise Turkish from Arabic or, I don't know, Hungarian? I don't have any contact details.' Jessica gestured towards the bagged iPhone. 'Check yourself. I am not supposed to be seeing her. She is a bit, suffocating, sometimes. She just appears when she has something to tell me to do. Apparently, she is a bad influence, I am not sure people really understand Lideri; she can act ... odd.'

The detectives sat quietly, watching Jessica process her thoughts. Perhaps she was heard acting out her dream in Turkish – if she even knew enough Turkish words to shoutout in her sleep. She would ask Jason if he heard anything. He sometimes records her funny, sexy, or happy sleep talks, playing them back to her in the morning. His ringtone for her is a recording of Jessica singing in her sleep. Her eyes stung, she wanted to go home to Jason.

'Please just ask my husband. He was with me every second of the evening, including when the shots fired. I even took him into the bathroom to pee.' She blushed again, finding it easier to direct this information to the kindly Mahatma, rather than his stern colleague. 'It will break Jason's heart if you mention Sumer.'

'Mrs Taylor,' Mahatma spoke, extending a kindly and reassuring hand across the table, 'we are in the business of serving and protecting. We are not looking to break hearts – we leave that to unfaithful spouses.' She lowered her face staring at his hand, less than an inch from her own. 'But you will assist us in every way you possibly can, to catch this murderer, and if you deceive or obstruct me, you will be charged and imprisoned.'

He did not wait for her response, but she nodded anyway.

Indira spoke. 'Do you have antihistamine tablets Mrs Taylor?'

Jessica was anxious not to incriminate herself or any of her friends. She consciously waited a moment following each question to think carefully – even before answering a seemingly innocuous enquiry.

'Yes. I am sure you have found them in my room. For hay fever, and to calm my eyes and throat in the spice market. But only half dose; they make me very drowsy.'

'You have high levels of chloroquine in your blood?'

'Yes. Antimalaria. I missed a couple of nights, so I took four tablets in just under twenty-four hours.'

'Do they affect you? Confuse or cause hallucinations?'

'No, not really. I dream more perhaps, but I already dream often. *Confuse*? No, not really.'

You have extensive bruising around your bottom and hips. Have you been in a struggle?'

'I slipped over in my room before all this happened and, as you know, I slipped heavily in Troy's blood.'

Indira studied Jessica's face when responding to her questioning. Her own expression was completely blank, neutral, but her eyes bored into Jessica's eyes, seemingly scrutinising her soul.

Mahatma placed a manila folder onto the table, bearing a Turkish flag, Turkish embassy seal and, jandarma crest on the cover.

'You are quite the decorated hero Mrs Taylor. And a good shot.'

'I was in the wrong place at the wrong time. I was involved in a terrorist incident. I did what I did and they thanked me for my efforts. The Turks gave me a gong. It isn't a vocation of mine, but shit happens around me, sometimes, so it seems.'

Mahatma tidied the desk.

'You have been most helpful Mrs Taylor. Do you want to ask us anything?'

'Am I under arrest? May I return to the UK?

'No and I am afraid no, Mrs Taylor. You are a person of interest, and we ask you stay in Kerala and keep my office informed if you sleep anywhere other than your hotel.'

'Hobson's choice?'

'I am afraid so. You will understand this is a horrendous crime of international relevance.'

'I can't go back to my room wearing a hazmat paper suit.'

'Of course. We will find you something from our lost property fashion boutique.'

'Why was Mr Singh in the Anderson's room?'

Both detectives sat back in unison. Indira spoke.

'We cannot discuss operational matters.'

The three held a long silence, broken by Mahatma.

'We are on the same side Mrs Taylor, and I need you to step up with the queries I have left you, please. I cannot leave threads hanging that may unravel a future case.' Jessica nodded. 'Ok. Mr Singh is also under arrest. As the soldiers battered the bedroom door, following the shots, it was your Mr Singh who opened the bedroom door from inside, to let us in. He claims to have smashed the window, to gain access from the balcony – but we cannot corroborate that fact, at the moment.'

'Yes. I did hear the window smash. Did he use his nightstick?'

'He says he used his nightstick, but we are struggling to corroborate that fact. There are shards embedded into the nightstick, but that could have happened after the window was smashed. The glass is thick, solid, and tempered; it would have taken some force to break it. If, say, the window was smashed from the outside, then the outside glazing pane would shatter and fall mostly outside onto the balcony, because the inside glazing pane would still be intact. Then when he smashed through the inside glazing pane, those shards would have fallen mostly inside the room. And vice-versa if the window was smashed from inside. So, Scenes of Crime are having difficulty establishing if the window was smashed from inside or outside – with the fairly even distribution of shards both inside and outside. Did you hear the glass break before or after the shots?'

'It must have been after the shots because I was sat on the floor, singing.'

'Singing?' Jessica shrugged. 'But it was not the shots that first woke you?'

'I need to think Mahatma, sorry. Maybe the person on the balcony woke me first. I may have dozed again, sitting up at the desk, I am not sure. I get confused. Then the shots, immediately afterwards. Then the glass breaking. I am so tired.'

Did you hear shouting before the shots? Possibly in Turkish?'

'Yes, I did. But it was only a dream. How could you know that?'

The detectives glanced at each other.

'And neither Singh nor Sumer were in your room at any point during the evening?'

'No.'

'Was your connecting door open – at any time during your stay? Was the bolt, lock or door ever opened?'

'No! May I visit Mr Singh and Sumer, please? Mr Singh trusts none of you and Sumer may be trying to protect my reputation and marriage. I could encourage them to speak more openly, perhaps.'

'We have you kissing and hugging Mr Singh on CCTV and we all know you have been rolling in the hay with Sumer. You seem to have vested interests in both parties.'

'I am offering to help, Indira. I believe both men are innocent and the sooner you catch the culprits, the better for them. But I am not trying to cover-up anything.' The three sat in silence, Indira waiting for her senior colleague to decide. 'Finally, may I speak with Zeynep and Diaz, please?'

'Ok Mrs Taylor. Here is my decision. Singh and Sumer may have a visit with you if they so wish. If you misuse anything they tell you, I will prosecute you for perverting the course of justice.

'Zeynep has been arrested and bailed for resisting arrest, threatening with a firearm, and illegally discharging a firearm in a way likely to cause injury to a public servant. Like yourself, she is also a person of interest in the assassination of the Canadian High Commissioner and the murder of Troy. Perhaps you will see her back at your hotel.

'Finally, Mrs Anderson knows where you are if she wishes to contact you.'

*

Indira escorted Jessica into the hotel lobby. The manager appeared and took her to the same low table she had previously sat with Sumer. Zeynep already sat at the table. She stood and grabbed Jessica into a hug.

'Sorry Jess. I could have got us all killed. I thought it was the soldiers who were attacking us. I was so confused.'

They sat together, hands, arms and legs entangled. Jessica looked towards the rooms. Hers, Zeynep's and the Anderson's stood cordoned off by exhibition boards, decorated with photographs of the hotel, the spice market, and the world-famous Chinese Fishing Nets.

'Ladies, please. You may not return to your luxury rooms. When the police have finished, our builder must start.' Zeynep's hand shot to her mouth. 'Please. We can find you a lovely room in a neighbouring hotel in Fort Kochi, or Kochi Main Town. Or I can offer you a standard room here at Branston Wharf Boutique Hotel.'

'I want to stay please if you also stay Jessica. Please stay.'

The manager cleared his throat.

'Sorry miss. We only have one standard room available. You can imagine, our availability is … stretched.' He gestured to the crime scene.

'We will share a room, until another becomes available.'

'Yes Mrs Taylor. Of course.' He glanced at Indira and back to the women. 'The police released some of your belongings. I will have them taken to your room.'

Jessica and Zeynep looked to Indira, for explanation.

'Standard procedure. We have kept your laundry, towels, bedclothes etc. We also have your journals, your phones, and laptops. We have kept your medicines and your first aid kit, Zeynep. I am sure the manager here will help you liaise with a pharmacy for replacement medication. We have kept some documents, Zeynep.'

'No! I need my medication. And some documents are highly confidential and personal, relating to … to the High Commissioner's Office.'

'Here, Zeynep.' Indira handed her a white sealed envelope, bearing a police crest. 'The police surgeon has written an emergency prescription for your replacement specialist medication. The local clinic holds the drugs, they are expecting you. Again, I am sure the hotel manager will assist. You will need to contact the High Commission and inform them of the documents you are worried about. They will approach us directly. We will copy, process, and return everything we can. Some objects we will keep as evidence and probably eventually archive. Your receipts are with your released belongings.'

Indira left the hotel, the manager left to arrange for the belongings to be taken and unpacked in the second-floor double room.

'At least the upper rooms have private balconies!' Both women sniggered.

'This is the second bed we have shared Jessica. I have only ever shared a bed with two lovers in the whole of my life, but two with you already!'

They laughed again, both conscious onlookers might find them crass. Jessica would have preferred to move to a large, anonymous business hotel.

'Jess, I am sorry to ask. Why did you tell everyone I had a knife to the children's throats?'

'I did not! I was worried the soldiers would see you had Mr Singh's Kirpan and that would put you in more danger. It is why I pushed you away.'

'But I did not have his knife, nor any knife.'

'Yes, you did. I saw it Zeynep, I felt it in your hand.'

'No, I did not. Obviously, Scenes of Crime would have found it. I did not have a knife, you are mistaken.'

'I … I don't know what to say. I must be confused.'

'The police also say you deny having Lideri visit you last night. Why are you saying that? I heard you arguing.'

'No Zeynep. I was … messing with Jason, my husband.'

'In Turkish?'

'No, I don't think so.'

'I spoke with Diaz – the police told her a second witness heard a woman shouting in Turkish.'

'No. I must have been dreaming.'

'Troy said you are friends with Kurdish separatists. You must tell them about Lideri, Jess.'

'I have told them all about Lideri. But she was not here last night!'

'Ok Jess. Ok.' Zeynep bowed her head, rubbing her temples.

'How are the kids?'

'Diaz says they are both awake, but drowsy. The children and I were drugged with antihistamine – no damage done, just drowsy. The police believe it was added to our milkshake powder – the children and I always have a warm milkshake together before bed, a tradition. I guess that saved them from the horror of the situation. God, I miss them.'

'And Diaz?'

'She returned from her meeting just as the shots fired. The police wanted her to stay as a person of interest, but she is already back in Canada with the kids, under diplomatic immunity. Unfortunately, diplomatic immunity doesn't quite stretch to third national au pairs. But to answer your question, she is broken.'

*

'Sorry Zeynep, I have a meeting.'

Jessica moved to the high table and sat on the stool, logging into the hotel workstation. Rani, the company therapist connected.

'Hey, Mrs Taylor.'

'Rani. Look, I have some stuff going on. Can we reschedule, please?'

'Sure. What sort of *stuff*?'

'Where to start? You have heard about the Canadian High Commissioner? It all happened here, in my hotel. Guess who is *a person of interest*.'

'What? You are joking! Jessica, what happened?'

'I don't know, exactly.'

'*Exactly*?'

'I am worried Lideri is involved.'

'Jessica, you need to get Legal involved, now. I can refer you.'

'I don't want to escalate the situation …'

'When did you see Lideri last? In India?'

'I am not sure Rani. I am so tired. Yes, in India. But I'm not sure when. I am worried she was in my room just before the High Commissioner was shot. I am not sure, I thought it was just a dream.'

'Ok. I don't want you to worry.' Jessica scoffed. 'You need to ask Company for legal representation. I will talk to Dr Cindy Stockholm on Monday. Has Lideri got you to do things, recently? Anything?'

'I am not sure. No. Nothing really. I have a friend she doesn't like. A guy. But I make my own decisions, not Lideri. He has been arrested. I am visiting him tomorrow, in jail.'

'No Jessica. You must not become more involved than you already are.'

'Sorry Rani, we need to reschedule this session.'

Jessica disconnected Teams.

*

The women moved to their new room. Housekeeping unpacked their clothes.

'You know whose room this is Jess? This is Troy's room.'

'No! I had no idea. Oh well, we know how it became available.'

'Is that a joke?'

'No! No, of course not. Sorry.'

Zeynep opened the double wardrobe and inhaled the air from inside, closing her eyes and savouring the scent. She sat on the edge of the bed and pushed a dent into the pillow, lying alongside as if sharing a pillow with the invisible man.

'I need to have reception reset the safe combination. It seems to still have ... an old number set. Not that we have our passports to keep safe any longer. This place is crawling with police and military intelligence. It is probably the safest place in India.'

Zeynep punched a number into the safe, opening the door. Checking the inside was empty, she set a new number.

'5-8-9-1. Your birth year back to front, Jess. This place was supposed to be secure on the night some random guy, or guys, wandered in to take two lives.'

Jessica decided not to query how Zeynep knew her birth year, nor Troy's safe combination. Zeynep took a pair of large sunglasses and a floppy hat, to sleep in the shade by the pool.

*

Jessica dialled home from the room phone; Jason answered.

'Jessica! What the fuck? Are you ok? Jess?'

'Jace, don't swear at me. I need …'

'Jess! I have had the police around. Special Branch. Christ, why didn't you answer your phone?'

'Please don't shout. The police have my phone. Calm down or I will ring off.'

'Are you ok?'

'Yeah. Honest. I want to talk about our date night. Ok?'

'What?'

'Did you hear me arguing with Lideri? Shouting in Turkish?

'Yes. You were nattering as usual, in your sleep. Then I heard you arguing in Turkish, just after you went to see who was on the balcony and before the shots. I was worried it was you and Lideri talking. I would say arguing though, not shouting. You know, not like screaming shouting. And you were singing in Turkish after the shots.'

'And you must tell the police that we were on our Teams date for the whole time. Yeah? I was with you when the shots were fired. Yeah?'

'Sure. But Jess?'

'What?'

'Obviously I will tell the police I was with you, when the shots were fired.'

'But?'

'No buts. I need you home.'

'But?'

'Jess. You went on to the balcony and did not come back to me. Half an hour later, maybe an hour, I don't know, I was dozing, I heard the shots. I guessed you were off camera, because of your arguing voice, but I couldn't actually see you. But that doesn't matter. What matters is, I will tell them we were together when the shots fired.'

'Shit! Exactly what do you remember? Exactly!

'You woke me. You shouted out *Mr Singh* or something. Then you said you were going onto the balcony. I heard you arguing in Turkish off camera. I heard a lock and bolt, I guess from inside your room. Then I heard the gunshots. I heard a window or glass breaking outside your room. I heard another lock being operated, louder. You told me to be quiet. I heard singing in Turkish, was that Lideri, or you? Then the Teams ended.'

'What? An hour? I must have dozed again; I was a bit woozy from the malaria meds. Jace, what if Lideri …'

'No Jessica! Lideri - *nothing*!'

'I need to sleep. Sorry. Sorry for everything.'

'Jess. There is one more thing. I recorded our Teams date, to watch later.'

'I know. You always do. Pervert.' She forced a giggle.

'Special Branch have my laptop. They might pick up on you being away when the shots fired.'

*

Zeynep sat on the edge of the bed. Jessica lay, fully clothed.

'Hey sleepy. Goodness, you chat in your sleep.'

Jessica sat, taking the coffee.

'Sorry. I must have crashed.'

'Indira is waiting in the lobby, to take you to see Sumer and Singh. Jess, you don't have to do this, you owe them nothing.'

'It was my idea.'

Zeynep rubbed her hand along Jessica's arm.

'Let's get you showered and changed.'

*

The prison sat on Kochi mainland. The walls proud and pristine. Inside the outer gates, the landscape changed into a bleak environment of dust, high fences, and barbed wire. Zeynep talked Jessica out of wearing the summer dress she had worn to seduce Sumer; instead, she wore an office trouser suit. She carried two bags of clothes, toiletries, fresh food, and tinned fish. The guard took her to the conjugal suite to await Sumer.

'Shit, Sumer! What happened?'

'I walked into a door. Thank you for asking Mrs Taylor.'

Jessica hugged Sumer, until he flinched with the pain. She helped him sit on the sofa, taking the stool opposite.

'You got us a room alone.'

'The police arranged this visit, Sumer.' He shrugged. 'I am here to promise you my support, and to ask you to be honest, and defend yourself. You do not need to protect me.'

Sumer shrugged again. He dropped his gaze; Jessica took both his hands.

'I am guilty of many things, Jess. Many things that will be the end of me. And I am guilty of falling in love with my boss. But I did not kill the Canadian. You can take that straight back to your policeman friend.'

'May I ask what happened in Branston Wharf on Friday night?'

'I will tell you, Jess. Repeat as much of it as you like. I thought your Canadian friends had left the hotel. I thought you might let me take you out for a walk, maybe. Perhaps you might ask me to stay in your room for the night. The Sikh let me into the lobby, but the receptionist refused to call your room. She said I should call from my own mobile; I texted you. I sat in the lobby. You did not answer. I wandered to the pool to see if you were stood on your balcony. Then I heard a female shouting and the gunshots. I thought someone had shot you. I ran towards your room, but there were soldiers everywhere. I ran back to the pool and shouted up to your balcony. The police say the Sikh saw me climbing on the balcony structure, but I don't remember. Later, I woke in a military hospital, with concussion.'

'Do you have a lawyer? Can I phone your family?'

'One thing my family is not short of, Jess, is criminal lawyers; they are sorting something. But thank you for asking.'

'Did a soldier hit you? Did he shout a warning? You should complain.' Sumer gave an incredulous snort. He met her eyes - his own bloodshot and blackened. 'Troy did, and the Indian police still do, believe you have a motive. And the police know you had opportunity – or at least you were in the immediate vicinity of the murders. I don't want you to admit or deny anything to me Sumer, I am just telling you *as it is*. You told me Cameron should be *made an example of* to warn off the protestors. Protestors who are trying to cost you and your family a lot of revenue. Protestors from a lower caste standing up to you. You must find that quite … disrespectful.'

'What do you understand about any of that? You are just a stuck-up, white English girl, preaching to me about things you have no idea!'

The couple stared into the gap between them. Jessica had never been accused of being *stuck-up* before – or even *white*.

'Regretting your bit of brown boy on the side, Jess? All a bit embarrassing?'

Jessica stood, without making eye contact and walked to the door, knocking for the guard to let her out.

'I regret nothing Sumer. That is rude and unfair. My offer stands: please contact me if I can help.'

Sumer scoffed and continued to stare ahead.

*

Zeynep waited across the road from the prison gates. A concrete bus and coach terminus with taxi rank, carpark, and a few cafes, serviced visitors, staff, and professionals attending the prison, and the occasional released inmate making their way back into society. Indira arranged for a squad car to drop them at the prison, finding their own way home. Jessica flopped into the plastic chair opposite her friend. The Chai Wallah brought a hammered-out steel plate of Aloo Bonda, with glass cups of milky sweet tea, smelling of ginger and liquorice infusions.

'Your boyfriend ok?'

Jessica returned a glare, Zeynep blushed. Jessica sipped her tea, dunking the hot crispy balls of spicy potato into the shared bowl of coriander chutney.

'My colleague is beaten, bruised, and accused of murder. Otherwise, he is fine.'

'Did he do it, though?'

Jessica studied her friend. Her eyes also red and puffy, but from crying.

'Darling, I know Cameron and Troy are family.' She allowed the comment to hang.

Neither spoke for over a minute. Zeynep sipped her chai, watching Jessica work through the pile of Aloo Bonda and chutney.

'Do you know who introduced tea to Britain, Jessica?'

'Oh, quiz time!' Jessica smiled broadly, grasping the opportunity to lighten the mood. 'Um. India.'

'Nope, other way around. Britain introduced tea to India, from China. Now they drink nearly one-million tonnes of tea each year. Britain wanted to break China's tea producing monopoly. A couple of years ago, I picked *Indian* tea in Turkey, helping to break India's monopoly.'

'No! Really?'

'Ok, question two and three. Who introduced coffee to the Italians and tulips to the Dutch?'

'No idea. Arabs?'

'Nope. Turkey.'

Jessica managed a grin of surprise.

'Are you making this up, Zeynep?'

'Nope. My point is, Jess – reality may not always match your preconceptions. Everything doesn't need to fit your understanding of the world. Sumer and Singh have motive and opportunity, working together or separately. If they murdered my friends, my adopted family as you say, then you should not invest your emotional strength and effort trying to vindicate them – just because you have soft spots. Let it go Jess, let the police do their job, don't interfere. On behalf of Diaz and the children, I am saying your running around arguing for them is … offensive. Ask yourself why you direct your concerns towards Sumer, instead of towards your own husband.'

'I am here today with police blessing. I don't want it to be either of them. But I do want them both to speak out, in their own defence, and tell the whole truth.'

Jessica tried to ignore the comment about Jason – she would not allow this younger woman to rile her.

'Troy is, was, no fool. He saw through them both. They did this – one or both did this.'

Jessica watched Zeynep tense, shoulders rise, her neck tighten. Tears filled her eyes. The couple stared at each other.

'It is very kind of you to be here for me today, Zeynep. But you should have stayed at Branston. I do not mean to offend the memory of your friends, but I do not regret offering these men my support, for what it is worth, in return for them having to listen to me ask for the truth.'

'How very British *fair-play-stiff-upper-lip* of you! You lot just love an underdog. Just remember Jess, an underdog is still a dog!'

Zeynep called for more chai. Her eyes wide and darting.

'I will speak to Mr Singh shortly, yeah? I won't be long. Then we can head back to the hotel. Shall we put a call through to Diaz and the children? They will love to speak with you. They will just be waking – if they slept at all.'

Zeynep relaxed a little, nodding away her tears.

'Last quiz question, Jess. Where was Chicken Tikka Masala invented?'

'I know this one Zeynep. That tasty, wholesome Indian dish was invented in Britain. Your point being?'

'My point is, Jess, I am not saying everything from Britain is bad.'

Jessica smiled, squeezing Zeynep's hand across the table.

'But you pushed and kicked me as I tried to protect my ... the children and you falsely accused me of having a knife to harm them. Now you think you are clever in trying to get these murderers off! Get your priorities sorted, girl, or you will be making some high-powered enemies!'

'Oh, for goodness' sake, what is it with the mood swings, Zeynep? Are you now threatening me? Directly or via Diaz? You are the one who needs to take the chill-pill, love! 'We have already been around the *knife* buoy, and the reason why I kicked you away as you swung a loaded gun around a room full of soldiers and a top politician! You should thank me for stopping you from being shot! Now get off my case. I mean it Zeynep, enough!'

*

Mr Singh walked unaided into the otherwise empty visiting room; hands and legs chained. He walked taller than the previous few days; a hidden weight removed from his shoulders.

'Don't tell me Gurdit, you also walked into a door?'

'Ha! Mrs Taylor! My favourite guest from Branston. I hope you are having a lovely day, so far.'

Jessica stood and hugged Mr Singh. The guard did not intervene. They sat opposite each other, across a narrow steel table, bolted to the floor.

'I am guessing that nice police detective has sent you to see me. Not that I mind; you appear most decorative to this old man, in such a dowdy place.'

His eye held a mischievous glint; he smiled. Jessica reciprocated and held his hand across the table.

'My idea, but yes. Mahatma likes the idea of me visiting you. He wants me to talk you down from that proud high horse of yours and to cooperate with the investigation. Which makes sense Gurdit – you are in the frame; you do realise that? You are a politically motivated, active, separatist, harbouring a grudge against the Canadian High Commissioner, who was then found pumping out blood in a room, which you opened the locked door of. The only person who survived that room was you. You have shedloads of motivation and opportunity.'

'Goodness gracious, Mrs Taylor! I must remember to tell my lawyer not to call you as a defence witness. But now I must ask you about your accomplices. I saw your friend Sumer escaping the scene, and I heard you chatting with your friend earlier. Then I heard your mystery friend screaming, just before the shots. It sounded to me, as if from right inside the Anderson's room.'

'Lideri?' Jessica scoffed. 'I doubt that very much! But first, what do you mean Sumer was escaping the scene?'

'Just between us two?'

'No, Gurdit! If you tell me something connected to the murders, I absolutely will report back to Detective Mahatma. And so should you. This is why I am here – this is not about some political ideology debate. This is the murder of a family man, his colleague, and about you wrongly taking the blame!'

'Ha! My dear Mrs Taylor, ideology? Really? Thousands of young Sikhs fought like lions, and died, to protect England from Germany in two world wars. India occupies my homeland in the Punjab, and my concern is purely ideological? If Germany ruled England after the war, would your predicament be ideological? If India recognised German sovereignty over the UK, would you see that as a decision of different ideologies?'

'I didn't mean …'

Singh squeezed her hand.

'Mrs Taylor. You tell who you like – it is your conscience. Yes, I saw Sumer half over the balcony, clambering down the cast iron pillar. I invited him to wait for the police to arrive.'

'With your nightstick?'

'Indeed. I had more pressing matters to worry about. Guests of Branston Hotel were in mortal danger. Whilst the Indian army politely knocked on the bedroom door, with shoulders and rifle butts, I gained entry through the balcony window. Breaking the tempered double glazing was the easy part – clambering through the window was trickier, with my old hips. My plan was to lean through the broken window and open the balcony door from the inside, but it was deadlocked and the key missing. As we say in India, there is no fool like an old fool.'

'You are no fool Gurdit, and the bravest lion I have ever met.' A shiver ran down her spine – she had once called her old lover a lion and he returned the nickname – shortly before betraying her. 'So, if the balcony door was deadlocked from the inside, how was Sumer escaping?'

'Good point Mrs Taylor. Good point. There is no access to the lock from the outside. Perhaps he was climbing up the balcony, to visit his Juliet, not down the column as I had assumed.'

Jessica nodded, deep in thought.

'Gurdit, I want you to explain how you could have heard someone you thought was my friend Lideri. Let us just say, for argument's sake, it could not have been Lideri who you heard arguing, especially in the Anderson's room. Just accept, for this argument, it could not have been Lideri.'

Singh shrugged.

'Our security hero Troy was most interested in your elusive Kurdish friend. He was worried how Lideri was able to keep slipping past reception unseen. According to Troy, you mistook Mrs Anderson for this Kurd, right outside the

Anderson's balcony door on the day you met Diaz – my own receptionist repeated to me the questions Troy had asked. You definitely spoke her name in an argument as I passed your room earlier that night. Then I heard her, or someone, shouting in Turkish perhaps, or at least not in English or Indian, just before the shots. Two plus two, equals …'

'Three. You are not the only person to hear her, Gurdit. Zeynep also heard us arguing earlier and Lideri shouting before the shots. But I know …, I just know. Have you told the police about Lideri?'

Singh laughed, a deep, genuine, throaty laugh.

'Mrs Taylor! Should I keep information back from the police, or not?'

'Gurdit, the connecting door to the children's room - was that open, closed, locked – when you smashed your way in?'

'It was definitely closed and locked, Mrs Taylor. I went straight to the bedroom door and unlocked it for the soldiers, before trying the children's connecting door and being promptly arrested. The bedroom door mortice key shares the same welded metal ring as the balcony door deadlock key and bedroom door night latch – same as your set of room keys. The bedroom door mortice key was still in the big old mortice lock of the bedroom door, with the other two keys dangling from the keyring.'

'But the mortice key for the connecting door was not on the same keyring?'

'Not exactly Mrs Taylor. But shall I let you into a Branston secret? The mortice lock key for the Anderson's room 101, the children's room 102, and your room 103 are all the same. And those same keys fit both the connecting doors between the Anderson's and the children's rooms, and also between your room and the children's room. The big old brass key is more for decoration. That is why there are heavy bolts on both sides of the connecting doors. And why there are unique secondary night latches fitted to the bedroom doors. The latches, with a deadlock fitted, to the balcony are also unique and secure. Just not the old mortice locks.'

'So, when the Anderson's took two rooms …?'

'We issued a separate mortice key for the connecting door and unbolted both sides – but the mortice key is surplus. They could have used the bedroom door mortice key – should they need a little, private, adult time – or used the bolt. I also told Mrs Anderson when we issued the extra key.'

'Gurdit, have the police kept your kirpan? Not your old one, but your new ceremonial knife?'

Mr Singh stood, lifting his shirt to show the small knife tucked into the waistband of his prison trousers.

'The first night they took my shoelaces and belt from me. But let me keep my kirpan and turban!' He laughed at the absurdity.

'Did you have it with you, the whole time?'

'Yes Mrs Taylor. Why do you ask?'

'Mr Singh, you are looking more like your old self. Even taller, even stronger, even younger.'

'I have fought a good fight for a very long time. But I was feeling my age, feeling *impotent*. But not anymore Mrs Taylor. I have pretty, young women asking to visit me, police officers queueing up to hang off my every word, and young prison guards thinking they are braver than me – they are not. I battered my way into that room to help protect the guests under my care. But, if as a result, people take notice of me again – then so be it. There is still fight left in me, and in the Punjab.'

'Gurdit, promise me you will not let pride get you into more trouble, please.'

Mr Singh gave a booming belly laugh.

'That nice British border guard said something very similar to me Mrs Taylor, the day I was expelled by Britain for inciting acts of terrorism abroad. *Abroad* being my own country!' He boomed more laughter. 'If you promise to distance yourself from that Brahmin of yours, Mrs Taylor, get yourself nice and fat to return home to your husband – I will see what I can do about the pride I feel as a displaced Sikh.'

Chapter Ten

'Mrs Anderson. How are you? How are the poor children? I am just so sorry.'

'Jess. I assumed you were Zeynep calling from Branston's guest email address. And it is Diaz, please. I think we have been through enough together, to drop the formalities.'

'Zeynep is sleeping. But she is desperate to talk to you. To you all. Especially the children …'

'Jess, I am going to stop you there.'

Diaz leant forward, into the camera. She had aged. Her eyes ringed red. Jessica saw the heads of the children snuggled into the duvet of their mum's bed. Diaz angled the camera away.

'What can I do for you Jess?' Jessica went to speak, but Diaz continued to talk over her. 'I was not accidentally blocking your calls from your own email address.'

'No. I realised …'

'Jess. I can never thank you enough for how you stepped in to protect the children and then Zeynep. But I just cannot do this, right now.'

'No. I understand …'

'Why Jess? Why the fuck are you protecting those two men?'

'I … I promise I am protecting nobody. Has Zeynep told you that? The police agreed I should ask them to be less, … awkward …'

'Less fucking *awkward*! Christ! And the police say you still are not taking them to your precious Lideri. What Jess? What the fuck?'

'It isn't that I am not, Diaz, honestly. It is not that easy.'

'Not that easy? I tell you what is *not that fucking easy,* Jess! Having your children's father blasted through the heart, that is what isn't *that fucking easy*!'

'I shouldn't have contacted you Diaz. I am sorry.'

Diaz sat back in her seat, looking to the side, and pinching the bridge of her nose.

'So why did you call, Jess? I would have contacted you once the police have finished.'

'I honestly think something is seriously wrong with the investigation, Diaz. I am not saying it couldn't be Mr Singh or Sumer – but things don't add up.'

'Like?'

'I know Troy is like family. How long have you known him?'

'I knew him before I met Cameron. It was Troy who introduced us. Troy and Cameron were best buddies. Troy was involved in the NGO work I was doing. So, what doesn't add up?'

'Troy was found holding a gun. Two men, alone in the room were shot dead. Doesn't the finger point towards, you know, the guy holding the smoking gun?'

'I thought you and that senior detective were best buddies.'

Jessica shrugged for the camera. Diaz turned to study her screen; Jessica maintained eye contact with the camera lens. Diaz shook her head.

'The bullets, which killed Cameron and Troy, are likely the same as those issued to Troy. Or at least the same calibre.'

'Ok.'

'But the bullets passed through the soft tissue of both men.' Diaz gulped and squeezed the bridge of her nose again, harder. 'The bullets are completely distorted by impacting the stone walls. So, the police are struggling to confirm Troy's gun was used in both, or either, murder.'

'But – doesn't the evidence suggest …'

'It looks like only one round was fired from Troy's gun: the magazine otherwise full. Only one round is missing from the magazine. Only one casing recovered from the scene. My husband's last moments, our bed, is now just *a crime scene.*'

'Um. Sorry. Only one, plus the round Zeynep fired by mistake?'

'No, Jess. Only one. Including the shot fired by Zeynep.'

'Are there any, you know, patterns and residues?'

'Troy may have residues consistent with discharging his firearm, but nothing conclusive. The problem being

Zeynep fired the gun with it still in Troy's hand. Blood splatters are all over the place. Cameron's body does not show any signs of firing anything, if that is what you are asking.'

'No, of course not.'

'I am out of here Jess. If your Detective Mahatma was on the ball, I would not even be having this conversation with you. And do me one favour, please – I can't face Zeynep just now. Keep her away from me. I want to start rebuilding my children's lives. I need space.'

'I promise to talk to Zeynep. But she is far from ... binary, with her thinking.'

Diaz scoffed.

'Whatever. And don't you contact me again. We can talk, maybe, once the perpetrators are behind bars.'

'Wait. Diaz, sorry. Look, what was the whole Troy and Zeynep thing, going on?'

'Not what you think, Jess.'

'But they looked so, *intimate*.'

'Not what you think, Jess.'

'And the DNA tests?'

'What did you say? What do you know about DNA tests?'

'I just happened to see ...'

The screen died. Diaz had closed the session.

*

'Darling, it is nothing personal. She just needs space. By the time this is sorted, and you can start your new life in Canada, Diaz will be ready to see you. I promise.'

'You promise? Like you have some influence.' Zeynep turned away on the bed. Jessica cuddled behind her; Zeynep did not resist the contact. 'You don't understand Jess, those children are like my siblings. They are the only family I have left, along with Diaz.'

'Zeynep, I have an appointment with Mahatma this afternoon. I am going to hand-in Lideri. Snitch on her. Hand her over. But I promise you, she is not connected with this.'

Zeynep turned her head to study Jessica's face, now looking down on her. Jessica brushed hairs from Zeynep's cheek.

'About time.'

'But I want to explain other things to the police as well. It has been thirty-six hours since the murders and the police are still chasing their tails. I want to fill them in on Troy and Cameron's relationship. They need to understand how and why you were all so close, so thick. Once they understand the skeletons, they can build a picture of events that do not involve you and me, so we can both go home. They need to finish investigating Singh and Sumer, hopefully releasing one or both.'

'And take your friend Lideri out the frame? How convenient.'

'Exactly. Tell me what was going on between Troy, Cameron and Diaz. Tell me about you and Troy. Tell me about the children and the DNA tests. Your mood plummeted the day you received the DNA results. You cringed when Cameron gave you a hug on returning to the hotel and you totally shunned Troy, let alone bitching at me in the taxi.'

'What about the DNA tests? You are a million miles away from the mark Jess, you are talking rubbish. If you continue spreading rumours and gossip about the Andersons and us, you will only slowdown the investigation.'

'I am not taking your advice, Zeynep. Either you explain what happened with the Andersons and you both, allowing me to give the police your version, or I go to them with all of my concerns as I see them. Let's start with the DNA tests, shall we?'

Zeynep turned away, her cheek back onto the pillow. Confusing her for Lideri, for a moment, Jessica moved to give her a reassuring kiss to the shoulder before halting.

'I explained about the DNA samples of the children for identification purposes.'

'Let's not play games Zeynep. You slipped in two other tests, didn't you?'

'You cannot tell anybody Jessica, I will lose my job … Ok, I guess that is no longer an issue, but I cannot risk repercussions.' Both women sat up on the bed, facing each other. 'Promise?'

'Go on Zeynep. I am not trying to get you into trouble, but this situation is not going away, and the police have the DNA results.'

'But not the names for the sample donors, they are anonymous! Even I don't really know which is who's. I was given the authorisation to provide samples of the children, as requested by the Embassy and the Royal Canadian Mounted Police. It is considered an intrusive procedure, taking the sample swabs, and I have that authorisation – like with changing nappies and kissing grazed knees. But I slipped in two other swabs, which I am not authorised to provide. Looking back, I should have just used an online clinic.'

'One was yours? And the other?'

'Troy.'

'Troy? Why Troy? Is this all connected to the children?'

'Damn Jessica, of course not! Are you spying on me? Why are you saying this stuff – are you trying to get me hanged?'

'Calm down Zeynep. This needs managing, and I am your best bet.'

'It is not what it seems. I thought Troy was my father. I was guessing, hoping, the results would prove Troy is my dad.'

'Troy agreed to provide a sample?'

'God no. I *accidentally* swung one of the children around and punched Troy in the lip. While I was cleaning the cut, I took a swab.'

Jessica's eyes widened in surprise as she brought both hands to cover her mouth. Zeynep blushed.

'You poor kid. So Troy isn't your father. You must be devastated.'

'Not really. I fantasised my stepfather was really my dad, then my uncle. Even Boris Johnson.'

'Boris Johnson! The disgraced British ex-prime minister?'

Both women laughed again.

'Well, he has Turkish heritage and seems to have fathered plenty of other children.' Zeynep shrugged. 'Oh well, lesson learned. I need to stop hoping every nice, older man, is my dad.'

'Boris! Nice? But you have to kiss a lot of frogs ...'

'Yeah. But I now have my Canadian citizenship. I need to start looking forward, not backwards. The Embassy has sent me a very odd invitation to apply for the role in the Personal Assistant's office in the Canadian Embassy to Turkey. My au pair position is coming to an end with one month notice – they have told me to apply immediately. I need to stop chasing father shadows around the world and make something of my life. You see how this DNA thing could ruin everything?'

'Sure. Let me think about it. But?'

'What?'

'The results suggest the third person is also related to the first two, presumably the children.'

'I know. It must be a mistake or contamination. I can hardly ask for a retest.'

*

'Hello Mrs Taylor. It is very good to see you again. How is your weekend?'

'Not brilliant Mahatma, to be honest. I am feeling very sad about what happened, and I am not sleeping well. Poor Zeynep is distraught, as you would expect.'

'We were expecting you to bring someone along with you.' Indira spoke.

'Sorry? Should I have brought a lawyer?'

Mahatma spoke again.

'Goodness Mrs Taylor, not at all. You are one of the team.'

Jessica detected a slight, self-deprecating blush from the detective. She also detected a slight eyeroll from his colleague.

'We understood your *missing* friend, Lideri, was to accompany you and help clear up a few loose ends.'

'I need to explain about Lideri.'

'No Mrs Taylor – Lideri needs to explain about Lideri!'

Jessica looked to Mahatma for support. He glanced at his watch.

'Let us hear Mrs Taylor, Indira. Mrs Taylor, you have one minute to explain, then we need to look at the possibility of your withholding information.'

'Even if you are *part of the team*,' Indira added, less helpfully.

'My friend, Lideri, is very important to me. We have been through a lot together.' Jessica motioned towards the empty area of the desk, which previously held the Turkish file during her original interview. 'But I must explain.'

Indira let out a long sigh.

'The thing is, Lideri is not like us,' Mahatma placed a calming hand, palm down on the desk, to silence his colleague, 'in so far as, she is dead.'

'Dead, Mrs Taylor? I am very sorry to hear this.' Mahatma glanced at his colleague. 'And are we, the police, aware of this development?'

'It happened some time ago. A few months ago.' Jessica stared Indira in the eye, daring her to smirk or roll her eyes again. The return expression was largely neutral, with just a hint of concern.

'Do you still see her often, Mrs Taylor?' Indira spoke. Jessica shrugged. Mahatma looked between the two women.

'Sometimes.'

'On the night of the shooting?'

'No, not really. I don't think so. It can be confusing. Sometimes it is a dream, sometimes the dream fades, and other times it does not fade. Sometimes she is real, when I am awake – I can feel her, taste her skin. Well, obviously not *real* in the *real* sense of the word. That night I might have dreamt about her, but she wasn't actually with me.' Jessica shrugged again.

'Does she tell, or ask, you to do things?'

'Sometimes. Mostly, she is just disappointed when I do something wrong. She didn't like an airline pilot I met, or Sumer. Or Jason. She gets jealous, I guess.'

'Did she dislike the Andersons?'

'I am not sure. Shall I ask her?'

Both detectives glanced towards the empty *lawyer's* chair next to Jessica. Jessica roared with laughter, holding both hands to her face.

'She isn't here now, obviously! What, you think I am crazy or something?' She continued to laugh – so infectious, the two detectives had to join in.

*

Mahatma walked Jessica to the front desk of the police station. The uniform had stepped forward at the end of the interview, but Mahatma waved her away.

'You have something else on your mind Mrs Taylor.' Jessica shrugged. 'It is best you tell me now. If you tell me before I find out, it is a reason. If you tell me after the fact, it becomes an excuse.'

'Fancy a beer detective?'

'Our canteen does a lovely chai, Mrs Taylor. They have a breakfast tea as English as the Queen, or a lovely Assam Tea from way up north.'

They sat in an empty corner of the canteen. The serving lady brought over two black teas and a plate of puff pastry Chaat Bites. She winked at Mahatma who responded by tapping the slight bulge of his belly and returning a satisfied grin.

Jessica studied the man – his closely shaved scalp, large, round friendly eyes, slightly bulbous nose holding up his round wire glasses, and two rounded, protruding ears to match the spectacles. Probably not much older than herself, he had the kind, smiley face that would one day win him a glamorous grandpa competition. Jessica suspected he had a very happy, lucky wife – who fell in love with his gentle personality, rather than any classical good looks. He smiled, she blushed.

'Sorry Mahatma. I was miles away. Back home in England, perhaps. I have a very kind husband. I have enjoyed India, but I think it is time for me to return to him. He doesn't fully understand Lideri, neither do I, but he accepts she is real – real to me. Soon I will say a final good-bye to her. Whatever Indira thinks, Lideri could not make me do something bad, against my will.'

'Indira is an exceptional detective and police officer, Mrs Taylor. There are well over 1.5 million officers in the Indian Police Service – if we all got together for a party, they would have to house us in a city bigger than your Birmingham. Indira is one of just a handful of women who will reach the top ranks.' He smiled to himself. 'Don't tell her I said this Mrs Taylor, but one of my career ambitions is to serve under her one day. One day, before I retire, I want to be calling her *Boss*. Put your trust in her.'

Jessica nodded.

'As we are on the same team, Mahatma, may I ask something? Only one shot was fired from Troy's gun. How were two men shot dead and one round misfired by Zeynep, with just one round fired? And I understand the balcony door was deadlocked from the inside – the key safely located on the keyring hanging from the bedroom door, which was also deadlocked, and mortice locked from the inside. So, my other question is, was the connecting door to the children's room definitely locked?'

It was Mahatma's turn to nod.

'Most salient, Mrs Taylor. This information stays *in-house*, please. We will, of course, disclose it to Singh and Sumer's lawyers when appropriate, but I would rather they hear it from us. Yes, the connecting door was indeed mortice locked from inside the Anderson's room with the key left in the lock, but not bolted. That connecting door was also bolted from inside the children's room; Zeynep is certain she had not bolted the door at any time - before, during, or following the incident.

'The pistol rounds are also odd. Singh's old service revolver has not been recovered but holds the same calibre .40 Smith and Weston round as is held by Troy's Beretta Storm automatic pistol. If Troy's automatic pistol was used, we would have expected to find two ejected shell casings, plus the one from Zeynep's misfire. If Singh's revolver was used, we would not expect to see the casings, as they are retained in the revolver cylinder.

'Now, I must ask you something. Has Singh ever mentioned where he keeps the pistol, as he is not permitted to wear it whilst the Canadians are staying? He is not being very … cooperative. And do you know if Singh has access to room keys? And, if I may be so bold as to ask, have you given Sumer a key or access to your hotel keys?'

'Mahatma! You know full well Mr Singh has master keys; I think you are testing my team loyalty.' She widened her eyes playfully, in mock indignation. Mahatma inclined his head in acknowledgement. 'And I have seen him use them to gain entry to my own room when I screamed in my sleep.

Sumer has never been in my room, nor did I give him a key. Whatever your smart Indira may be telling you – don't overthink my relationship with Sumer. We have had a couple of moments together, a holiday or office fling. Once in his hostel, once on the beach. I invited him for afternoon tea at the hotel and I now understand he made his own way there, once more, in the hope of ..., of seeing me again. End of.'

'And you have never left your keys with him?'

Jessica made a show of thinking hard, before answering. Mahatma detected a slight blush, Jessica broke eye contact.

'Um. What can I tell you, Mahatma? Unless super Indira has already sleuthed and rushed to tell you, the mortice key for all the bedroom doors and all the connecting doors is the same. One key fits all – hence all the secondary locks and bolts.'

'No, I ..., we were not aware.'

Sensing she had an advantage, Jessica pressed on.

'And how would Sumer having my night latch door key, or my balcony key, which is useless from the outside, even help him to gain access to the Anderson's room? The connecting door between my room and the children's room is bolted, on both sides. Follow the evidence Mr Detective – not your preconceptions.'

Mahatma playfully slapped his own wrist

'I stand, or sit drinking tea, corrected, Mrs Taylor. You remind me of my partner – always keeping my imagination in check.'

Mahatma sat further back in his seat and studied Jessica for a few minutes. She could see he was thinking of telling her something new. She waited.

'Ok Mrs Amateur-detective. I will now tell you something else, which Indira also *rushed* to tell me.'

Jessica steeled herself not to overreact to this new piece of information. She remembered how Jason and she played strip poker when first dating. She had trained her expression to reveal as little, or as much, as suited her game plan. She offered Mahatma one of her more sickly-sweet smiles.

'We are perplexed by the fact that the connecting door between your room and the children's room was only bolted from your side. It was not mortice locked, nor bolted, from the children's room. Again, Zeynep is certain she had not unbolted or unlocked the door from her side. I doubt she even realised her bedroom door, or connecting door, key would fit. It seems only you knew this intriguing fact. Only *you* knew you all had a key which fits the interconnecting door between your room and Zeynep's. You and, presumably, the concierge as a trusted keyholder.'

'The Andersons were told when the connecting door mortice key was issued to them. But you see that trail of crumbs leading to me, or Sumer, escaping the Anderson's room, bolting the connecting door from the children's room side, then bolting the next connecting door, from my own room side. Are you saying the perpetrator made their access and egress through my room? Or that I am the perpetrator? But don't forget the Anderson's connecting door was mortice locked from inside the Anderson room.'

'Or Lideri, perhaps? It is only a theory we are looking to discount. For instance, Mr Singh could have locked the Anderson's connecting door once *Lideri* had fled. Mrs Taylor, the soldiers were searching a seemingly empty children's room immediately following the shooting. You entered and found the children in a drawer under the bed. What made you look there and not, say, in the wardrobe as a more obvious place to hide?'

'I am not sure. I had a dream, where one of the children was in a drawer. Perhaps … Look, I really don't know.'

'And Lideri did not tell you where they were?'

'Mahatma! Enough with this Lideri nonsense, already! Lideri was a brave, brave young soldier. Not a murderer.' Mahatma raised a hand in acceptance. 'Just a thought, Mahatma, could the shots have been fired from outside? Smashing the window?'

'Meaning your Mr Singh lied about smashing the window with his nightstick?'

'Or leaving two neat bullet holes – lost when Mr Singh smashed the window? Or through the open top vent? Was the vent window open?'

'I suspect that is a little fanciful Mrs Taylor. You would have to be very tall to shoot through the vent window. But I shall have Indira check the scene of crime photographs and run some models on shooting through glass panels. You may just have supplied ulterior motives for Singh smashing the window and Sumer clambering around the hotel structure.'

*

The office supplied Jessica with a new laptop, iPhone, and sim cards with new telephone numbers. She had no access to work servers but knew her friend's email addresses in the Portsmouth office, downloading contacts, passwords, and photographs from the iCloud. She Teams called Jason.

'Hey. How's Brian? And you, obviously?' She gave Jason a flash of her cheeky grin.

'Better now, from hearing your voice. The dog couldn't care less.'

Brian took that opportunity to slobber over the screen, trying to lick Jessica's face and making both his owners laugh.

'I have told the police about Lideri. I couldn't have them waste more time chasing ghosts.'

'And you took legal advice, first? Right, so you didn't take legal advice, first? How will this look, Jess? You ranting to a dead terrorist, moments before the guy in the next room is assassinated. I tell you what, don't ever do as I suggest, will you?'

'Hey, easy. I don't rant, and she is not a terrorist.'

'That's it, Jess. Start defending her, see how that goes down.'

'I am not defending anyone. I am on the police side. One detective even admits I am *on the team*.'

'And the other cop doesn't? Like good cop – bad cop?'

Jessica felt herself blush with embarrassment.

'I am not stupid, Jace.'

'So don't act it! What did they say about Lideri? Have you spoken with Lideri since the shooting?'

'No. They are interested in Lideri …'

'I am not surprised.'

'But they aren't saying much.'

They sat in silence. Both smiled at the cameras at the exact same moment.

'And your Turkish friend? Zeynep, I mean, not the dead Kurd.'

'She is all over the place. The commissioner's wife is blanking her. She is me as well – but they are so close. Thick as thieves.'

'In what way? Have you told your new policeman friend?'

'I have nothing to tell him, yet. Zeynep may have had an Oedipus Complexion thing going on, but I am struggling to see why any of that should lead to Troy shooting Cameron. But then there is no reason why Troy should hide the ejected shell casings, before shooting himself. And it wouldn't have been easy to hide the second casing, after shooting himself in the heart.'

'Which all points to that other guy, Mr Singh, being involved.'

'Don't you start on poor Mr Singh. He did not break into the room and coolly shoot two men, one an armed ex-military policeman, before hiding a whole revolver. Mind you, he is refusing to say where he keeps his revolver. And he is the only surviving man from that locked room.'

A ferry sounded a long blast on the ship's horn as the superstructure filled the view outside Jessica's top floor bedroom. A tiny open fishing boat beeped a return signal as it scrambled out of the way, dragging heavy collapsed fishing nets. Jessica clearly saw sailors running along the deck, shining torch beams into the water as the boats narrowly avoided collision.

'You'd love India, Jace. We must come back here together, one day. Maybe a different hotel.'

Jason laughed. 'Yeah, maybe. How long will you remain a *person of interest*? When are you coming home?'

They both ignored the Indian elephant in the room, that Jessica may even be arrested or bailed as a suspect.

'It could be as long as 30-days, unless, you know, they have a reason to keep me here longer; or Lideri, if you see what I mean. But I am positive Lideri is not involved. I was a bit tanked up on anti-malaria medication, but I am almost positive I would have remembered something. And let us keep remembering, the room was locked from the inside.'

'Unless your Mr Singh helped you escape?'

'Shit Jace. Don't. That is what Mahatma said.'

'I am playing devil's advocate Jess. Of course, you are not involved. Other than you being involved in everything that ever happens within a ten mile radius. Why couldn't you have stayed in your room and let the Indian Army sort things?'

Chapter Eleven

'Jessica, I am not one to be threatened and bullied. I have spat out bigger fish than you!'

'Diaz, please. It is not a threat. With everything you have gone through already, I did not want to go to the police behind your back. You can help me to understand, or I can tell them what I already know. Honestly, it is whatever suits you best.'

'You can be a prize bitch, Jessica! That is like me saying: you tell me why you slept with a murder suspect, or I ask your husband what he thinks.'

'Have a go ruining my marriage Diaz, if that is what you want. I seem to be giving it a good go, on my own. But this is about one or two innocent men facing the death penalty.'

'They appear to have very little on your two friends.'

'But they have even less on anyone else – except Troy. Surely, we all want the truth out. Or is that the problem here? The truth. You didn't waive diplomatic immunity to stay and support the police.'

'How fucking dare you? I brought my children home after their father was murdered in the next room. And for your information, you little bitch, I don't have the prerogative to waive diplomatic immunity – that is a decision of the foreign office, not mine. But you know fuck-all about any of this. Like a little knowledge – you are a dangerous thing.'

'I do not pretend to know the answers. If I did, why would I contact you, to be verbally abused? I am trying to help bring Cameron's murderer to trial.'

'Whilst hopefully *getting-off* one or two of your men who you have already *got-off* with!'

Diaz sat at an office desk, dressed for work. Jessica wondered if she already had a new au pair or nanny arranged. Diaz stared wide eyed at her screen – the look reminded Jessica of the rabid bitch, which she saw shot on the beach.

'How did you first know Troy? Were you together?'

'That's it, Jessica. To you, everything comes down to sex. You might look for validation by seducing every man you meet, but we are not all the same as you. We have a French-Canadian word for married women like you. It translates as *slut*!' Jessica sat quietly, waiting for Diaz to continue. 'Ok. I worked for an AIDS/HIV charity based across Africa. Troy still worked for the military police providing diplomat security for the consulate in the Congo.'

'And he also worked for your charity? How did that happen?'

'Worked? Not exactly.

'Troy had AIDS? Oh my God!'

'*Has*. Although I suppose you are technically correct, now - *had*. I had the police test your blood after the shooting, just to check you are still ok and suffered no infection. They didn't give you the results? Ha! Typical – completely incompetent! Well Jess, you are just fine. I am sure there will be plenty of men in the future, including your husband, who can give an unknown sigh of relief. If you want my advice, I should practice safe sex and take reasonable precautions – testing again in four weeks. Have you been sexually active since the shooting, two days ago?' Jessica ignored the snipe.

'Shit! And Zeynep? Was she tested, is she ok? She was flaying around in Troy's blood.'

Diaz stared back at her screen without expression. Jessica glanced at the bag of Zeynep's medication on the desk.

'Zeynep? How did she become involved with your charity?'

'Talk to her about that. The charity does lots of good work, supporting families and children orphaned by AIDS. We do educational programmes, support women's start-ups in African villages, where the male population is decimated by the disease. All sorts. But I am not talking to you about Zeynep specifically – that would be highly inappropriate. A good time to end this conversation, I think.'

'No, wait, please. How did you end up in Turkey?'

'You could find this information on LinkedIn Jess. You are just being nosey and wasting my time.'

'Please Diaz. I cannot let the police loose, grilling Zeynep about all of this. She is too fragile.'

'You think you are so clever. Do you see yourself as a young, alluring Miss Marple, manipulating and pushing buttons? I can see straight through you, you little cow. I wish it was you in that prison!

'Look, this is all public knowledge. Troy and Cameron met in the military police whilst based with NATO in Izmir, Turkey. Imagine, Troy is the simpering, silent type. Cameron is flamboyant, extrovert. Troy is chiselled, broad and strong. Cameron is pretty, vulnerable, unintimidating. Perhaps opposites attract. Cameron was a staff warrant officer – a junior military diplomat. Troy the crack military policeman.

'I recognised Troy at a consulate drinks party in Kinshasa, Congo. God, they were a couple of popular guys. Troy in his dress uniform, Cameron in his White Tuxedo – he had already moved to the diplomatic service by then. Troy waived me to the front of the admiring queue of women. We joked that the three of us were invited as eye candy. Heady days.

'Cameron was offered a diplomatic post back in Izmir, partly because of his previous deployment there with the military police and his smattering of local and cultural knowledge. He arranged for Troy to be posted back to Izmir in the role of diplomatic security expert, and me in the genuine role of new doting wife. And now I am his new doting widow and the doting mother to his bereaved children. Thanks in part, Jessica, to one or both of your manfriends.'

'Diaz, one last question please …' Diaz ended the call.

*

'I am having a bath Zeynep. I do my best thinking in the bath. Before I do, can I ask you a couple of things, please? I have an idea of how shots were fired through the open vent window of the Anderson's room.'

'Sure Jess. Ask anything.'

'Really? Thanks. Firstly …'

'No Jessica! I was being sarcastic. I thought you Brits held the monopoly on irony. I answer police questions only. I am sick of you asking me questions, to build a fake defence for your various lovers. I am going to the restaurant.' She slammed the bedroom door.

Jessica watched the passing ferry eclipse the sunset from the balcony; the passengers so close to her balcony that she carefully wrapped her short dressing gown around her naked body. Since taking an excessive dose of anti-malaria tablets with corresponding vivid and surreal dreams building by the night, followed by the earlier cruise liner dominating the view from her room – she now shuddered. A loud crack from the ferry made her start. She screamed and jumped back from the balcony balustrade.

Jessica saw two seamen securing a steel locker door; she laughed at her own jitters. She saw the security guard look up from the pool and give a wave. She missed Mr Singh and his reassuring nightstick.

She returned to the bathroom, lit a candle, and filled the bath. Years after she had backpacked around Europe and Turkey, she still never took a deep hotel bath for granted. She carefully measured half the bath oil into the running water, leaving plenty for Zeynep, before shrugging and tipping-in the rest. She turned out the lights and slipped into the bath.

'Zeynep? Is that you? Sorry I upset you.'

'Shush darling.' Jessica sat in the bath, to see Lideri stood naked by candlelight. *'You must not call me another girl's name, sweetheart. Especially one so pretty.'*

'Lideri! This is seriously bad timing. I need to think. Now bugger off!'

Lideri span around slowly.

'What do you think? Have you seen me naked before?'

'What do I think? I think you need to shave! Now, bugger off!'

'Shave? I am a Peshmarga Commander, not a high school cheerleader!'

Through a fit of giggles, Jessica pointed to the bullet wound in the middle of her friend's chest. Lideri shrugged.

'I am still a commander. Just a dead one.'

Lideri climbed into the bath, Jessica laughing too much to offer resistance.

'Don't leak into my bathwater!' Jessica gestured to the wound again. 'Does it hurt?'

'Do you remember the night I was shot? It hurt then. Does it hurt you to see it?'

'Yes, my love. It does.'

'Then it still hurts me, Mrs Taylor.'

'Please! If you insist on getting in my bath, stop calling me missus!'

Both women laughed together. Lideri straddled Jessica's legs, purposely scratching her with leg and pubic hair against her thighs. Jessica thrashed and recoiled, but the trained fighter had no difficulty in dominating her friend.

'Come on Jess. Tell me what you are thinking about.' Lideri brought her mouth to Jessica's and gave her a long kiss.

'Why did you kiss me?'

Lideri shrugged, sitting back in the bath against the opposite end, water poured and bubbled through the bullet wound.

'Why not? We love each other.'

'Are you kissing me goodbye?'

Lideri shrugged again.

'Talk to me Jess.'

'Lideri, did you kill the Canadians?'

'Oh! You English are so blunt. I would have bought you lunch and a thousand glasses of tea before coming to the nitty-gritty. Just come right-out with-it girl!' Lideri laughed as Jessica just smiled, studying her friend.

'That wasn't exactly a no.'

'The room was locked from the inside.'

'So, your whole defence revolves around the room being locked, which I, apparently, had a door key that fitted? Jason and Mahatma believe Mr Singh would have locked the connecting door, once I, or you, had escaped. Zeynep and Mr Singh say they heard you screaming in the Anderson's room.'

'Me screaming? Maybe darling, if we ever make love, you will hear me scream your name. But screaming at two men, before I shoot them – not my style. I am a soldier, not a bunny boiler. Ask your policeman friend about residues. I can't decide whether you are accusing Singh of assisting you or denouncing you!'

'There are gunpowder residues and blood splatters on my dressing gown.'

'I am not surprised. You were blood-wrestling that pretty Zeynep when she fired the gun. I would be more surprised if you hadn't some patterns. And her, no doubt. And Troy.'

'Doesn't sound like much of a defence.'

'No Jessica hanim. It is not. Do you know what my mountain warfare instructor once told me? No? He said: never eat yellow snow.'

The two women laughed again, Jessica spluttering white wine into the bath. Lideri went to kiss her again, but she resisted.

'I don't like this kissing Lideri. You are being too soppy. You mustn't leave yet. I want you gone, but not yet.' Lideri gave a thin, noncommittal smile. 'What else did your instructor tell you?'

'He said the best form of defence, is attack. Stop worrying about locked doors and open windows. ''Why' did those two men get themselves shot?'

'The victims are thick with each other, and with Diaz, and the gorgeous Zeynep.' Again, the two giggled, Lideri slapped Jessica's arm.

'You will not make me jealous; you teaser. How so?'

'Diaz and Zeynep are no longer singing from the same hymn sheet – but they are united in wanting the police to chase shadows.'

'They have something to hide?'

'A pretty powerful *something,* for two women of different generations, from two continents and opposing backgrounds - to unite. I asked if you did it Lideri, you still haven't answered.'

'No Jessica, that is a problem. Perhaps they each have something different to hide. Does that fool you married still hate me?'

'Jason is no fool, and everyone hates you.'

'Except you.'

'Except me. And get your dirty feet off my tits. When did you last wash them? The soles are disgusting!'

*

'Sorry Lideri, I dozed.'

The candle had burned out, the room dark. Hands grabbed Jessica's ankles pulling them upwards and sharply towards her head. Her head and shoulders slid below the water. She opened her eyes wide under the dark bubbles, screaming muffled into the water. A weight against her calves pushed her shoulders against the bottom of the bath. The taps turned on, cascading more water. Jessica found the rim of the tub with one hand, but the more she pulled against it, the more her body jack-knifed and flattened against the bottom.

Her grandmother would say she had found a giggle's nest and laughed at the eggs. The more impossible the situation, the more she laughed. She sometimes laughed at funerals. She once laughed as a lover slipped slowly towards a cliff edge. She stopped laughing, but her smile remained. She stopped breathing, her lungs full and warm, satisfied. She imagined Jason sat with Brian. Jason shook his head slowly, incredulously – *oh Jessica*.

The room was already dark, but the blackness deepened. She could not see the face of her best friend, but she knew the blackness was Amara's skin, her beautiful colleague of Nigerian heritage. She felt a lone bubble leave her nostril.

Chapter Twelve

A bright, white light penetrated Jessica's consciousness. She assumed she had turned over, looking at the bottom of the bathtub. As she stretched her arms to push herself up, so the whiteness moved further away. She held her breath, refusing to take another lungful of water. This would be her last effort. The hands were on her again, pushing her back under the water.

'Easy Mrs Taylor. Easy, easy, easy. You are ok. Breathe normally.'

An alarm sounded. She could smell perfume. Large, clear, beautiful eyes peered directly into hers. Jessica shouted Lideri's name, but the sound trumpeted into nothing. A choking, sharp pain ripped through her throat, sinuses, and chest.

'Let's pop this tube out people; job done.'

The eyes were back.

'Hold on Jessica, nearly done.'

A searing pain ran through her throat. Fire filled her upper body.

'Well done nurse. Cooking on gas. How about a little sugar air for the young lady?'

A plastic oxygen mask hovered menacingly between the eyes and Jessica, before clamping against her face.

'How are we today, Mrs Taylor?'

A tall lean man bent over Jessica, replacing the beautiful eyes. Jessica nodded.

'Who is the prime minister of Great Britain, Mrs Taylor? Only joking. You are just dandy.'

Jessica smiled. Her eyes closed slowly, like the flapping blind in Sumer's hostel room.

*

'Mahatma.' Jessica croaked. 'Have you been here the whole time?'

Mahatma looked embarrassed, not having been available to sit by her bedside.

'Not really, Mrs Taylor, sorry. It is not every day the Canadian High Commissioner is murdered on my patch. But my timing is impeccable. I arrived at your hotel room, just as Zeynep was opening your door after dinner. I think we found you just in time.' He held up a hand to stop her speaking. 'Rest your throat, Mrs Taylor. The doctors will keep you here for twenty-four hours, to monitor for secondary drowning. But you will be just fine. The doctor is more worried about the reason you blacked out. Nothing is showing on your scan …' Jessica squeezed his hand to silence him.

'I was attacked. Someone tried to murder me.'

The beautiful eyes appeared in her view again. Indira spoke.

'Who Mrs Taylor?'

'I could not see. Dark.'

'You seem to have no real injuries. A little bruising around your ankles and under your arms, where Mahatma and Zeynep pulled you from the bath. Your back and ribs will be sore from the compressions, but no other obvious injuries. You are fortunate, Mahatma has just completed his compulsory first-aid refresher – after dodging it for so many months.' Indira glanced reproachfully at her boss. 'Are you sure you were attacked, Mrs Taylor? Not dreaming or hallucinating? Could it have been Lideri?'

Jessica shook her head, snorting a scoff.

'I'm sure. Not Lideri. She only tries to save me from … myself. She only ever saves me.'

Indira brushed stray hairs from Jessica's face.

'Mrs Taylor, I am not arguing with you, especially just at this moment. We have further researched your association with Lideri. She did not always look after you. She kidnapped and nearly murdered you.'

Jessica shook her head.

'You don't understand.'

Mahatma spoke.

'Not now Mrs Taylor. It doesn't matter.'

Jessica nodded and tried to sit; Indira helped pull her up. Under the sheet, Jessica wore only a cotton shroud tucked around her chest – allowing the doctors access to the front of her body. She moved a foot from under the sheet to study the bruising. She had two intravenous drips fitted – she assumed one was fluids, and one antibiotic to prevent or fight a lung infection. She would ask, later. Zeynep sat at the end of the bed, wringing her hands, and looking very concerned. Jessica smiled and nodded a *thank you*. Sumer stood inside the door, holding a bunch of tulips – looking frightened. He made to move towards Jessica, but Indira held up a restraining hand. He skulked back against the wall.

'Shall I send them both away, Mrs Taylor?'

Jessica smiled at Indira's bluntness. She was beginning to like her. Jessica shook her head. Zeynep stood, glared between Jessica and Sumer, before stomping out of the room.

'Darling, I think you should sleep now.'

Jessica nodded a reply to Lideri and closed her eyes.

*

Sumer held a glass to Jessica's lips, the intravenous drips and monitors removed.

'I like being pampered, Sumer. But I am fine, honest.' She held up a glass medicine bottle with a spray attachment. 'This is a local anaesthetic for my throat. But I keep biting my numb tongue.'

Sumer smiled at her hoarse giggling. He kissed her lightly on her lips and then on her forehead.

'Sorry I told you off for being stuck-up, Jessica. But you are, a bit.' She slapped his chest.

'Thank you for the tulips, my favourite. Do you know who introduced tulips to Europe?'

Sumer ignored the question.

'They released me from prison, as you can see. They have no reason to hold me – they just wanted something to tell the press, and the world. *Brahmin Boy Turned Bad*. But even these corrupt peasants need some evidence.'

'Surely Indira and Mahatma are high caste?'

'Mahatma is almost certainly a Vaisya. Petty, money orientated *business-wallah*. Indira might be a Kashmiri Pandit. But we are all equal now, Jess. As I said, you cannot understand.'

'Mmm. That is not quite how you made that point, last time you said it.'

Sumer looked at his hands but fell short of apologising.

'How did you know I was here, in hospital?'

'I was waiting for you in the hotel lobby.' He gestured to the tulips. 'The receptionist refused to call your room and I do not have your new number. So, I waited. I walked around the pool, carrying a bunch of tulips, as you were drowning in your room.' He shook his head, to himself. 'Then all hell broke loose. They must dread me coming to see you.'

'Can you remember, on the night of the shooting, did Mr Singh have his revolver on him?'

'The first I remember of Mr Singh, is his nightstick smashing my scull. And to be honest, I don't really remember that, either. Just what the police told me.'

'Did you hear Lideri, or me, shouting in Turkish from the Anderson's room?'

'I did hear a female screaming in a foreign language, not English, before the shots. But I never got to see who she was.'

'Arguing, or screaming?'

'Screaming. But from inside a hotel room.'

'And did you hear the shots? Were they fired from inside or outside the Anderson's room?'

'I was by the pool, waiting for you to acknowledge me. I heard the shots, but I do not know where they came from.'

'Three shots?'

'No, two. Close together.'

'Sumer. Zeynep brought a bag for me. Help me get dressed.'

*

The replacement hotel concierge met Jessica and Sumer at the courtyard gate, glaring at Sumer. Jessica linked her arm through his and pushed briskly past, towards the lobby. Mahatma, Indira and Zeynep sat waiting at the low table.

'Sorry, that took longer than we expected. Thank you for meeting us here.'

'You had to stop off at Sumer's on the way?' Zeynep spat out the words. Jessica ignored her.

'Not a problem.' Mahatma offered.

'As you are *part of the team*.' Indira added.

'You have some information for us, Mrs Taylor? I understand you have worked out how the two men were shot.'

Jessica sat opposite Indira, nodding. Zeynep detected a smug expression on Jessica's face, she rolled her eyes. Jessica smiled sweetly, studying each face around the table, all eyes fixed on her.

'It is a shame Mr Singh is not here, to receive his immediate apology from the Indian Police Service.'

'I can assure you, Mrs Taylor, his release will be arranged in record time once we hear your deliberations.' Mahatma smiled.

'I cannot say why, or who shot the two men, that is yours to ascertain. But what I can do is explain *how* they were shot, and where to start looking to identify the hitman.'

Jessica looked around her audience. Sumer hung on her every word, concentrating. Zeynep looked nervous, wringing her hands again. Mahatma had the wide-eyed expression of intrigue – he reminded Jessica of Brian her dog, trying to understand how Jason could make the rubber cat squeak. Indira looked bemused – Jessica would soon wipe that look off her pretty face. They had all thought Jessica a little mad, talking to Lideri, but this was her moment to prove herself. For a few seconds, she allowed herself the fantasy of the Indian Police Service awarding her a medal *for detecting*, to keep company the one already awarded to her by Turkey. She cleared her throat. Her audience shifted forward slightly on their seats.

'The two shots were fired through the open vent windows, or possibly through the main bedroom window, leaving it otherwise intact.'

'Fired from where, Mrs Taylor?'

'From a passing ferry. Just check the timetable to see which one. Then check the passenger list for your murderer. We are all, including Sumer and Mr Singh, now clearly innocent of any involvement.'

Her audience remained silent and motionless – except for Indira, who snorted a loud laugh. She sniffed hard, wiping her nose and lip with the back of her hand. Taking her silent phone from her pocket, she glanced at the blank screen and squeaked to her colleague.

'Sorry sir, I had better get this, it might be important.'

Indira walked from the table towards the pool. Her head bowed and shoulders heaving in obvious but silent laughter. Mahatma had his back to Indira's exit; the other three watched her go. As Indira turned left in front of the pool and out of sight, the group heard her uncontrolled laughter.

*

Sumer gripped Jessica's hand. 'But …?' He could not think of a question.

Zeynep relaxed, staring at Jessica as if trying to understand a stranger speaking in an even stranger language.

Mahatma sat back in his seat, looking thoughtful and a little perplexed.

Indira marched back to the table. Standing tall, her hands behind her back and wearing her stern expression, she apologised.

'Sorry sir. For that. Sorry. My call can wait.'

'Sumer, Zeynep, please take a moment to relax at the bar. Detective Indira and I wish to clarify some of Mrs Taylor's thoughts, alone.'

Sumer squeezed Jessica's hand and slid closer. Zeynep took Sumer's lead, taking Jessica's free hand in solidarity.

'Move!' Indira shouted.

All but Mahatma jumped, startled. The receptionist and concierge looked over. Zeynep and Sumer walked to the bar. Zeynep took the stool furthest away from Sumer. Indira took her seat opposite Jessica.

'It is good to think out-of-the-box Mrs Taylor. It is what we need, at the moment.'

'From *our team*.' Indira added, a smirk crossing her lips.

Mahatma turned on his seat to face his subordinate and, for the first time, Jessica saw irritation in his expression.

'Indeed Indira. Better than using up precious work time taking amusing phone calls, wouldn't you say?'

Indira looked down at the table, embarrassed. She blushed scarlet, her ears and neck glowing. The smirk gone.

'Yes sir. Sorry sir. Sorry Mrs Taylor.'

Mahatma stayed silent, allowing his colleague to squirm in isolation. Jessica felt empathy towards the police officer, feeling her embarrassment. Jessica spoke.

'I am sorry I wasted your time, I guess …'

Indira spoke over her.

'Mrs Taylor, both men were shot at close range. They have gunpowder residue from the discharge, which suggests Troy was shot at point blank range to his chest, facing away from the window, and Cameron was shot from no more than a couple of meters away. You were not to know this, but it discounts your theory of shooting from the ferryboat. 'I, we, had not considered this possibility however and I thank you for bringing it to our attention – if only so it can be duly discounted. I would add that a *hitman* would have to travel the ferry many times to find a time when Cameron was in the bedroom with the lights on and shutters open. He would have no reason to shoot Troy, just to assassinate Cameron. Ballistic forensic suggests a .40 Smith and Weston handgun round, similar to that used in Troy and Mr Singh's …'

'Thank you, Indira. I am sure Mrs Taylor now understands how we would give such a theory as hers … due consideration.'

'God, I feel so stupid. I have watched too many Death in Paradise murder mysteries on television.'

'There are few officers in the service that weren't inspired to join by watching their favourite cop shows, Mrs Taylor. Don't beat yourself up.'

Jessica nodded.

'Mrs Taylor. I have some news. It is not good news, for you, I am afraid. We are close to formally charging Mr Singh with the murders of Mr Anderson and Troy. We have given Mr Singh every opportunity to surrender his pistol for forensic investigation, but he has refused.'

Jessica's mouth gaped, but she could not form any words. Mahatma continued.

'If we examined the revolver soon after the incident, we could establish, if fired, when it was fired. Or if cleaned, approximately when it was cleaned. The pistol could have helped convict or clear Mr Singh. But he is more concerned about publicity for his cause, than clearing himself. We are losing that forensic window, solely because Mr Singh will not cooperate, and we believe that is because he is guilty of the crimes.'

'Wait, no. Look … Let me think …'

'Mrs Taylor …'

'No wait. Why did Mr Singh lock the connecting door? It doesn't make sense.'

'To protect the children and Zeynep. We believe he also drugged them to make them sleep. He is an honourable, if not a desperately misguided man.'

'No Indira! How did he hide the revolver? How was the connecting door bolted from Zeynep's room?'

The two police officers glanced at each other. Indira offered the smallest of headshakes to her colleague, but Mahatma spoke.

'He has an accomplice. She took the revolver from Singh and disposed of it.'

'She?' Jessica shouted. Everyone in the lobby looked over. Zeynep jumped off her stool, staring at the group, wide-eyed.'

'I meant she or he.'

'Of for goodness' sake Hatti!' Indira lowered her voice. 'My colleague said *they* Mrs Taylor, not *she*.'

Jessica now spat her words out in stage whisper.

'The Turkish shouting was Zeynep? I don't understand. Zeynep was drugged and the connecting door locked from the Anderson's side. How did …'

'No Mrs Taylor. We think the Turkish was *Lideri*, well, you know, *you*. Scotland Yard are analysing your date night Teams recording, for us. But on first pass, we can identify the voice arguing in Turkish before the shots, as your voice.'

'I bet they are analysing it frame by frame. God how embarrassing.'

The detectives looked at each other again.

'In for a pound … We have every reason to believe Zeynep is not the accomplice.'

'What Mahatma? So that leaves me! Neither Zeynep nor I could have disposed of a revolver with half the Indian army watching!'

'We are not suggesting it is you, at this time, Mrs Taylor.'

Jessica threw her arms into the air.

'So that leaves the receptionist! I am voting for my ferry idea as the slightly less ridiculous theory.'

'No, Mrs Taylor. Not just the receptionist.'

'Sir, please. I want this on record, I am asking we stop this interview now and review our strategy, before proceeding. I am insisting, sir.'

'Oh my God! Diaz? You think Diaz hid the revolver?'

'Mrs Taylor. Indira is correct. This meeting is over, I may have overstepped the mark. I wanted you to do something for me, and for Mr Singh, and the families of the two men murdered, and in their memory. In trying to keep you onside, I have overstepped the mark and put this investigation in jeopardy.'

Jessica glared at the detectives, switching from face to face.

'Go on then! What? What do you want from me?'

'Mrs Taylor. Mr Singh obviously has a huge soft spot for you. You are the only one he doesn't sneer at or want to fight. He has refused to see any of his own family, discharged his brief and is refusing to see his Gurdwara Sikh elders. His separatist beliefs are spread across the world's press – he is going out with all guns blazing. Mrs Taylor, we have little forensics to prove him innocent or guilty, just circumstantial evidence, motive, and opportunity, if you can get him to …'

Indira spoke over her colleague and finished his sentence. '… tell us where the fucking gun is Jess. We only have a few hours left for this forensic window. We think he is guilty. You think he is not guilty. Prove it – get us the gun.'

Chapter Thirteen

'Ok Jace. It works like this. We have a reasonable conversation, and you control your temper. Or I cut you off. Deal?'

'What's up with your voice? What's happened now? Ok, ok. Deal.'

Brian glanced between his master and his mistress's face on the screen. He detected the tension, ready to do something endearing to defuse the situation, perhaps fetch the toy frog he was given on his birthday.

'Right. So, there was an incident, in my bathroom.'

'What sort of *incident*?'

'I drowned.'

'Drowned!'

'Only a bit. Stay calm. I spent the night in hospital. Sumer helped me discharge myself. All is ok now. See? Nothing to fly off on.'

'Summer? What does that mean? Who is Summer?'

'Um. It's a local expression. It means *with the weather on your side* or … Look, there is something else. The police think I had a blackout – which doesn't help with this whole Lideri thing.'

'Shit Jess, it can't get any worse. What? What is that look for?'

'It is a teeny bit worse.'

'Christ! How so?'

'Someone came into the bathroom and tried to kill me. Luckily …'

'Kill you!'

Jessica watched Jason's face redden. She leant towards the screen, a warning that she would end the Teams meeting if he shouted at her. Just off Jason's camera sat a low Turkish table, a steel tray on low folding wooden legs. Jason did not much like the table and Jessica was surprised it was still there. She knew it was there – because she heard Jason kick it across the room. On the table sat Jason's ugly hookah pipe, which she heard crash and break against the wall. Brian flew from view with a yelp. Moments later, Jason came back into view from screen right – Brian appeared screen left with his green *birthday-frog* clamped in his mouth.

'Sorry love. Go on. Are you safe now? Could it have been a blackout? How did you, you know, survive?'

'Luckily, the detective and Zeynep turned up at the room at the same time. Zeynep is a brilliant first aider and Mahatma has reluctantly completed his first aid refresher. So, I was in good hands. I wonder why it was Mahatma who stepped up? Anyway, *all's well*.'

'*All's well?* This isn't a *fuc* …, sorry. This is not an episode of Death in Paradise!'

'That is so funny Jace! I mentioned Death in Paradise to the police a while back! Amazeballs! Great minds and all that.'

'Where is the investigation going? When are you coming home? Have you a police guard?'

'Police think it was a blackout, I have no real injuries, which cannot be explained away by my *rescue*. Plus, I should still really be in hospital – so no guard. Which is handy, because I need to find Mr Singh's gun, to prove it wasn't fired.'

'*You need ...*'

'I am on the team Jace. I told you that. Also, and this goes no further. No further! But I think they suspect Diaz of disposing of Mr Singh's revolver! I know! I said there was something going on between the Andersons, Troy and Zeynep.'

'What?'

'I can almost see it. She went into the room with a warrant officer guard immediately after the shooting and just before Singh was taken away. Everyone would be looking at Cameron on his deathbed – she had the opportunity to take the gun and hide it in her bag or belt. Then she was whisked away to safety with the children – obviously without being searched. But there is a huge *but*.'

'Go on.'

'Mr Singh is such a sweet …'

'Oh for God's sake Jess! So where is the gun?'

'If, and this is a huge *if*,' Jason rolled his eyes, 'Mr Singh did shoot the two men and give the gun to Diaz, it is probably in some Indian landfill or on the bed of the Arabian Sea. But, and this is the more likely *but*, as Mr

Singh is innocent the gun has been stored safely somewhere. The cantankerous old git just needs to tell the police where, and soon!'

'Jess, you need to let the police find the gun. You, anywhere near the murder weapon, is not a good look.'

'Agreed. But where did he keep it? My guess is the hotel would have told him to get it off-site as requested by Troy while the Anderson's were staying. And he lives on-site. His family live in the Punjab. Surely any friend keeping it would have made themselves known, once they realised Mr Singh was arrested. He was always off on his motorbike, perhaps he buried it somewhere.'

'Unlikely. If he is attached to the bloody thing, he is unlikely to stick it in the ground. And what if a child found it? I am assuming it is only the gun missing?'

'Yes, I assume so. I know he was also told *to lose* his Kirpan.'

'Kirpan?'

'A dagger that all Sikhs carry.'

'A dagger? Bloody hell Jess!'

'It is only a ceremonial dagger. They carry them in the UK – even in airports. He probably left it at the temple.'

'Why not …'

'The temple! Jace, sorry I'm tired. Bye.'

*

Zeynep sat in the lobby, to allow Jessica to Teams call Jason from the bedroom. Sumer sat on the barstool.

Jessica breezed past reception, towards the door, clicking her fingers at Sumer.

'Where are we going?'

'Mr Singh's temple. Where is it?'

'How should I know?'

'It is close by. I saw him all dolled up and walking out some mornings – he never mentioned a lady friend. If it was very far away, he would have taken a rickshaw or his motorbike.'

'I know there is only one Sikh temple in Jew Town, close to the hotel. What's the book?'

'It is the Guru Granth Sahib. I borrowed it from the room.'

'You give every man in your life a stolen hotel book? Hey forget it, just teasing. This way.'

Gurdwara Road narrowed as it snaked inland from the ancient synagogue. Soon the buildings and bay windows overhead almost touched, blocking any light from the waning moon. Most of the businesses were closed for the night, Sumer lit the way by the torch light of his phone.

'Blimey Jess. I hope you are as scared as I am.'

A cat knocked a flowerpot from a dark balcony, Sumer jumped backwards into Jessica's arms with a yelp. Jessica doubled over laughing, clutching her sore throat. Narrowed Gurdwara Road opened onto a tiny square with two other exits. Two sides of the tiny square were little more than the corners of shops. Along the back of the square, and the longest unbroken stretch of building, stood Jew Town Gurdwara, painted a poor golden on the outside – Jessica thought it more Dulux Marigold in the poor streetlight. The double door stood open, covering much of the façade. Light and bonhomie spilled onto the tiny square.

'Why are we here Jess?'

'I am looking for something.'

'Not the gun Jess! Please, I cannot be seen anywhere near the murder weapon!'

'Oh man-up Sumer!' She mumbled *'bloody virgins'* under her breath. 'I am just checking where his kirpan ended up. He might be an old fool, but he is a proud old fool.'

'Just walk through, please.'

A young woman pointed to a reception room, a table set with paper plates and fruit. One end sat a delicious smelling curry, bubbling in a cauldron above a wax-candle heater. One of the surviving lepers Jessica recognised from Spice Market, sat at the otherwise empty table. She wondered if his remaining companion was still alive – and who now owned the cap. He waived.

'No, thank you. Well, actually, maybe, it does smell …'

'No! Jess, I need to, you know, be anywhere else.'

'Ok Sumer. Sorry, miss. I am looking for Gurdit Singh's, um, office. Room?'

The woman laughed.

'His tea chest you mean?' She looked pointedly at the book Jessica clenched to her chest.

'Yes. Gurdit is, away ...'

'We all know where Gurdit is. May I?'

'No. Thank you. He specifically asked me to leave this in his, his tea chest. Me, myself, that is.'

'Follow the corridor to the back entrance and wait there, please. I will have one of our very own Gurus attend, presently.'

They left the woman and followed the corridor to a steel door, opening onto a tiny square of yard. Before the door was an office, low energy lamps blazed. They sat.

'That is Singh's motorbike, in the yard, Jess.'

'Really? Yes, it is. Well remembered. I recognise the saddlebags.'

'I recognise the bike. It is an old Royal Enfield 500 Bullet. An old thumper. Military specification – or should I say relic. My grandad has one.'

'Your grandad rides a motorbike! I need to start seducing men of my own age. My grandad rides a Zimmer frame.'

'Jess, I still do not want to get involved. But ...' Sumer nodded towards a tea chest sat in the corner of the office, closed with a beaten metal lid.

Jessica opened the hinged lid to immediately reveal Mr Singh's long, traditional, Sikh Kirpan ceremonial knife. Wrapped in a protective cotton sheet was Singh's *temple-best* clothes. Under that, a stiff, large envelope with fancy writing in Punjabi and English – declaring Gurdit Singh's Last Will and Testament. Sumer stood nervously in the open door, watching out for Guru to appear. Below the envelope sat an open wooden box, made to slide neatly into the tea chest, containing old sepia photographs, a pocket watch, various knickknacks, and possible heirlooms. Jessica studied an old photograph of a beautiful, young, Salwar Kameez dressed woman, sat in an ornate, highbacked wooden chair. Behind stood a tall, beautiful, elegant older man in linen trousers, collar and cuffed formal white shirt, and wearing Mr Singhs long Kirpan tucked into a silk cummerbund worn over the shirt. In front of the woman stood a small boy, in formal shirt and *school* trousers – his uncovered hair tied into a high bun. The young woman wore a delicate silk turban of the same shade as her dress. The man wore a huge silk turban, adding size and dominance to his handsome, bearded face.

Jessica slipped the wooden tray out of the chest to reveal another identical tray containing documents and scriptures. Under the second tray lay Mr Singh's ex-army officer's, long nosed revolver, wrapped in a clean white rag. Jessica assumed the empty holster was in his room at the hotel security lodge, or probably now with the police.

Holding the pistol by the rag, she brought the cylinder to her nose and smelt for gunpowder residue. The ammunition magazine consisted of a rotating cylinder with an aperture for replacing the cartridges. Jessica used a pencil stub from the tea chest tray to rotate the cylinder – each section held a complete, intact, .40 Smith and Weston round; none were spent.

Sumer straightened and took a step along the corridor.

'Good evening and welcome. You have a book of Gurdit Singh's for safe keeping?'

'Yes, sir. Thank you for seeing us. My name is …, I am a friend of Mr Singh.'

'Ok.'

'Yes, I am fine. And you?'

The strange voice laughed from the corridor.

'I am glad you are fine. I guess I also meant – shall we step into the office?'

'Yes, of course. Shall we? Yes I think so. We shall.'

Both men looked towards the office door, at the sound of a heavy wooden tray hitting the floor and a female voice.

'*Fuck!*'

'After you then.'

'Yes. Thank you.' Sumer spoke again. 'It is just that Mr Singh also asked us to collect his motorbike and take it back to the hotel. Branston Wharf has offered to keep it safe until this, situation is, is resolved.'

'Really? That is good news. It is in our way, to be honest. We couldn't leave it on the road, but …' He tailed off.

'After you.'

Sumer crabbed sideways, obscuring the office door as he ushered Guru into the yard. Both men stood looking at the motorbike. Sumer cleared his throat, slipped his hands into his pocket and flexed onto the balls of his feet.

'Well, Mr …? There it is. Exactly where you saw it.'

'It is a lovely old bike.'

'A bit noisy.'

'Yes. It has a single 500cc …'

'Yes, I am sure it does. Shall we sort out this book and get on?'

Guru squeezed between Sumer and the bike, oil from the engine marking his long, flowing, white shirt - and into the office. Jessica stood in the middle of the room, clutching the book to her chest – arms folded into a cross.

'Hi! You must be Guru. Mr Singh has mentioned you.'

'Hello, and likewise Mrs Taylor. One of Gurdit's longer serving wards. You need to put his book with his other belongings? Yourself?'

'No, not really.' She handed him the book. 'Perhaps you could please, when you have a moment. I don't suppose you have an envelope and note paper, I could …?'

Guru gestured towards the wide, shallow drawer in the desk. Jessica shuddered as she slowly opened the drawer, peeping inside for any children from her dream, and from finding them and Zeynep in the blanket drawer under the bed.

She took a temple letterheaded envelope and notepad from the drawer and wrote a short note.

Dear Mr Singh,

I hope you are keeping well, and this old family photograph affords some comfort.

May I say: it is imperative that you cooperate with the police and tell them where your unfired pistol is stored. I respectfully suggest to you, Gurdit, that you no longer have a choice and if necessary, I will intervene on your behalf.

Love and respect

J x

She addressed the envelope to Mr Singh and marked it urgent, taking the liberty to add a return address on the back of the envelope on behalf of Detective Inspector Mahatma. She would call Mahatma presently, for him to follow up with Mr Singh.

'Come on Sumer, we need to deliver this to the prison without delay. Mr Singh will realise from the photograph that I know where the revolver is stored, but I would rather it came from Gurdit. Now he knows the game is up, he might come clean.' Jessica lowered her voice, speaking close to Sumer's ear.

Guru stood by the open office door to show them out, still holding the book.

'Come again, please. And eat with us or help with our work in the community. We are a man down with Gurdit ... away. We look forward to his speedy return. He is a good man.'

'Of course. Look, sorry, we must shoot – or perhaps I should say ... you know, just *get off*.'

'Um, sorry to interrupt. You have forgotten something.' Guru nodded to the motorbike.

'Yes! Absolutely I had not forgotten. It is the main reason we came. That and the …' Jessica pointed towards the book.

*

Guru remained in the corridor as Jessica and Sumer stood looking at the motorbike.

'Does it have a key?'

'I doubt it. Too old.'

'I will let you drive Sumer. It was your idea.'

'Um …'

'Don't tell me you are a motorbike virgin as well!'

'Please stop calling me a virgin Jessica!'

Guru cleared his throat.

Jessica moved to the front half of the old motorbike. She depressed the clutch lever with her left hand as she used her full weight to stamp down on the kickstart. It hardly moved. Jessica felt giggles bubble in her chest, she felt both men watching her. She hopped a couple of times on the stubborn kickstart, before bearing down with a jump.

The kickstart shifted, the engine released a single loud backfire and the kickstart propelled Jessica over the handlebars. Still clutching the grips, Jessica burst into giggles.

'Ow! That hurt! Right, I think I've got this.'

'Try this.' Guru stepped forward and eased down the decompressor lever, situated adjacent to the clutch lever.

Jessica tried again, this time the engine fired on the first attempt, the single cylinder thumping into life. Jessica shouted over the engine.

'Can you get the gate, please?'

She ran her hand along the handlebars before locating the light switches above each lamp holder, front and rear. She twisted the knurled brass switch, the lights pulsing to the rhythm of the idling engine.

With the gate open, Sumer climbed onto the pillion seat and grasped around Jessica's waist. She stamped the gear pedal down and released the clutch lever. The motorcycle jumped backwards, narrowly missing Guru and continued backwards into the corridor before stalling.

Jessica was now in uncontrolled laughter; both men looking worried. Unable to talk through laughing, Jessica gestured for the two men to bump the motorcycle forward, in gear, to align the crank, before starting the process again.

This time the bike lurched forward and through the gate, kangarooing down the narrow alley towards Kochi Prison. Guru waved goodbye as Jessica squealed and Sumer yelped to each forward jump.

Chapter Fourteen

'I know you don't want to hear this Zeynep. But I believe the police will have Mr Singh's revolver soon and ascertain it has not been fired. Where they find it, will suggest *no* accomplice. Hopefully they will release him and look for the real perpetrators or investigate how Troy was involved. It will also remove any suspicion from Diaz.'

'Diaz? Diaz is not under suspicion! What are you talking about? And you said it couldn't be Troy because his gun only fired once – he probably drew it trying to fight the assailant. You might not want to hear *this* either – but that revolver may well prove your Mr Singh *is* a murderer and there *is* an accomplice who removed it from the scene; perhaps one of the soldiers.'

'I am not saying … Look, Zeynep, I agree Diaz has no reason to kill her husband. And my, I mean the police, finding the gun where it is will demonstrate that no one is colluding with poor Mr Singh to commit any crime. Neither Diaz, nor a soldier, or anyone else would have any reason to hide the pistol. They would have just ditched it as soon as possible. I just hope the Canadians will allow Diaz to cooperate with the Indian police – maybe through the Mounties. She does such good work with the charity and everything. Is that how you met her?'

Zeynep shrugged.

'It is not a secret, I guess. When the Andersons moved to Turkey, Diaz mobilised an office for her charity, doing most of the work herself. Turkey already has a medical infrastructure, so Diaz set up nonmedical schemes to help families and young people affected by AIDS and other trauma. You will have to ask Diaz for the details, but there are clusters of AIDS/HIV infections and other Sexually Transmitted Diseases around NATO bases globally, including ours at Izmir. I guess North American soldiers contract disease from around the world and spread it to local girls. I think the Canadian Military and the Embassy facilitated Diaz's work, as they have a vested interest in helping the victims of these diseases. Presumably it is a good, responsible, public relations exercise.'

'Was your mother a victim of AIDS? Did Diaz and her charity sponsor you?'

Zeynep twirled her fingers through each other for a moment, watching the patterns created.

'Mum's Canadian boyfriend moved on deployment to Africa before they realised she was pregnant. He then paid for me to have antiviral drugs privately, when I was younger. I have HIV, Jessica, but I have never suffered a serious flareup. It is fully managed. I am not sure mum ever fully understood her disease, she always felt so fit and well. Anyway, she stopped taking her expensive Turkish provided medication, infected her new husband and my brother at birth, like she had infected me. So now, it is just me left.'

'Oh my God Zeynep. That is awful. And from the love-of-her-life – it must have felt like a cruel twist of the knife in her heart.'

'My uncle, the brother of my stepfather has a tea garden. He took me in after my stepdad died. When I started working for Diaz he sat me down, for a talk about the birds and bees.' Zeynep laughed. 'A rural Turkish, middle-aged bachelor, trying to give the sex talk to his step-niece. I am not very experienced Jess, but I know enough to realise most of what he said was incorrect. It was so funny. But he had every reason to mistrust and fear those involved with the NATO base, including Diaz, after what had happened to his brother, and to us all. He told me to be careful and relayed something my stepdad confided on his deathbed. Mum had been raped and he did not want me to *put myself* in harm's way; like it was mum's fault she *got herself* raped.'

'Oh No!' Jessica had smiled along with Zeynep's account of her uncle's ham-fisted attempt at the sex talk, but now her eyes welled as she grabbed Zeynep into a hug; as much for her own comfort as for Zeynep's. 'Raped by the Canadian boyfriend?'

'Goodness no, Jess. They were smitten. She was raped by one of the camp military policemen, following a dance she went to, with the boyfriend. It was the policeman who gave her HIV, presumably.' Zeynep shrugged. 'Anyway, whatever. Everyone knew of the allegation and where mum had caught the disease, so Diaz came looking for me, once she was posted with Cameron, to Turkey. First of all she helped with my final year of education. Then she found me a job as her PA's admin girl. Then, when they located to India, she took me as her au pair. Now she is trying to secure me the job as a PA back in the Canadian Embassy in Turkey. I owe her everything.'

'And the Canadian citizenship?'

'There is a scheme for foreign children of servicemen to apply for Canadian citizenship, but I had no proof my father was Canadian. Troy was there for me, along this whole journey. I cannot say for sure, but I think he pulled in every favour from Cameron, along with Diaz's support, to ease me through the system. I believe Cameron used his position to argue that the father should not be named for security reasons whereas, in actual fact, my father is really unknown.'

'And that is why you thought Troy was your father? Because he helped you so much.'

'Yes. And when I realised he also has HIV, it kind of made sense, but didn't quite add up. Just hopeful thinking, I guess. I wondered if he had slept with mum after the rape and caught the disease from her. But the dates don't really add up for that. The whole Canadian battalion, complete with the embedded 3 Military Police Company were on the move the following day – it was a farewell dance. My guess is the authorities – Canadian, Turkish and NATO were happy for the rape investigation to be derailed by the new deployment. The rapist probably realised he would be lost to a different continent before any investigation got going.'

'But you lost your whole family, to that rape.'

'I have said too much. I don't really talk about it. Only with Diaz.'

'Are you still receiving support for the trauma?'

'Jess, I just said, that is enough!'

Jessica nodded and managed a thin smile – no longer wondering why Zeynep's mood swung so violently.

*

'I cannot bare this waiting, Jess. I am waiting for the murderer to be found and charged. I am waiting to have my passport returned. I am waiting for my new job offer at the Canadian Embassy in Turkey to be confirmed. I am waiting to start the rest of my life. I really appreciate you agreeing to share this room at Branston, but I feel so imprisoned.'

The couple sat in the hotel restaurant, sharing a bottle of wine with dinner.

'I am desperate to go home as well, and I have suffered a fraction of your loss. I spoke with Indira. They visited Mr Singh last night and he has finally agreed to tell them where he stored the revolver – and so proving it has not been fired recently. I am worried this will actually extend the period for us to stay *persons of interest*, because the investigation is starting again from scratch. They can keep this going for thirty days, before they have to release us. At least they have dropped the firearms charges against you, Zeynep, *under the circumstances*. I am sure Canada applied some pressure – to assist the newest of new citizens.'

Jessica smiled at the young woman, who beamed back with pride.

'I just wish we were still on our rice-barge Jess. Our own world, away from murder and death.'

'It would be nice to turn back this clock; that's for sure. I'd be happier if I could go in to work, but the managers decided to implement my exit plan with immediate effect, not surprisingly. At least they have kept Sumer on, and he is busy.'

'Is Sumer, you know? Is he good?' Zeynep dropped her gaze to pour the wine.

'Oh, I don't know, Zeynep. He seems a good guy, but I wouldn't want to go into business with his family, that's for sure.'

'No. Well, yes. I see what you mean. But no. I meant, is he *good.*' Zeynep made a nonspecific gesture, flaring her nostril and flicking her head to the right. 'You know?'

'In the sack, do you mean? Zeynep! Are you getting the hots for Sumer? I thought you suspected him of …'

'Me? The hots for your seconds? I don't think so Jess. Ridiculous!'

'You so have! My goodness Zeynep, that is so funny.'

'Well, he is more my age.'

Jessica laughed, grabbing Zeynep's hands across the table. Zeynep blushed deeply and refused to make eye contact.'

'Oh well. If you aren't really interested, I won't bother answering.'

'Up to you. Doesn't bother me. I was just asking.' Zeynep concentrated on Jessica's hands, still holding her own. Jessica stifled her laugh. 'But you can tell me if you want.'

Jessica burst back into laughter. Zeynep tried to pull her hands free, but Jessica gripped them harder.

'Look at me Zeynep - when I am talking to you. I am enjoying this.'

Zeynep looked Jessica in the eye, shifting on her seat, and blushing still deeper. She raised both eyebrows, enquiring. Jessica leant forward on the table.

'He is fine.'

'Fine?'

'Inexperienced, but keen.'

'Keen?'

'He puts in the effort.'

'Effort? For himself or for the, … woman?'

'For the woman. Well, *this* woman, he did.'

'Do you think he would put in the effort, for me? If you have, you know, finished with him.'

Jessica's effort to stifle her laughter failed as she snorted a giggle – covering her mouth and nose with a hand.

'He isn't out to stud! He isn't a gigolo!'

'I am not saying …'

'He is a young colleague from the office. I can't just hand him over to you, like a …, I don't know, like the office stapler.' Jessica spoke through her laughter.

'Can't, or won't?' Zeynep joined in now, with an embarrassed giggle.

The waiters brought their meals, breads, and condiments. The women released hands and sat back.

'Take a shower cap – he has terrible aim.' Jessica continued speaking in front of the waiters, teasing her friend.

Zeynep snorted and spluttered a mouthful of wine back into her glass, coughing. The waiter rested her hand on

Zeynep's back, helpfully raising a spare napkin to her mouth.

*

Jessica knew Zeynep feared the dark. They started a bedtime ritual when sharing the double bed on the rice-barge, which now continued to the room at Branston Hotel. Zeynep kept the bedside lamp on until they were ready to sleep. She then turned it off, the women holding hands across the bed until they released their grip on falling asleep. Jessica understood how terrified, and brave, Zeynep must have been climbing into the drawer under the bed, to protect the children on the night of the shooting.

'I think we both need a distraction, young lady, and I am afraid it doesn't involve Sumer. I was thinking of booking another cruise on the backwaters – but our last trip would be a difficult act to follow. And anyway, I think we need a new adventure.'

'Anything Jess. Anything to take my mind off this waiting.'

'Have you an update on the new PA's job in Turkey?'

'Still nothing, Jess. What is the adventure?'

'Well – as you ask. Mr Singh owes me a little favour. If I hadn't persisted with finding ..., or should I say encouraging him to tell the police, where the gun was kept, he would now face capital charges. So, I think he should lend me his motorbike.'

Zeynep wriggled over to Jessica's side of the bed and peered into Jessica's face through the gloom of the night.

'A road trip! Yes, I love it. Where shall we go? We dare not go out of Kerala; we cannot risk arrest. No messing Jess, I know what you are like, I must not face arrest, under any circumstances. It would risk my job application, and everything.'

'We will let Indira know our route. We will stay in the west of the state. But I think we should spend a day going to one of the mountain Hill Stations and then, after a rest, continue to the Wild Lands and on to a tiger safari. Just a thought …'

'Yes! Tomorrow. We go tomorrow, Jessica.'

'Why not? You get one whole pannier saddle bag and half my leather barrel bag, strapped to the rear of your seat, for all your luggage.'

'I so need this, Jessica. You are such fun.' Zeynep planted a long, closed-mouth kiss on Jessica's lips, before snuggling against her chest. 'Shall we invite Sumer? We could sandwich him between us, on the bike.'

Jessica laughed into the dark, playfully slapping her friend's arm.

'He certainly gripped me very high, on the waist, as a pillion!'

Chapter Fifteen

'Thank you for the information, Mrs Taylor. We will keep in contact and may ask you to pop into a local police station or checkpoint. The best way to avoid us intruding, is to keep me posted, please.'

'Sure Indira, I understand. Zeynep and I are both going stir-crazy here. We never should have stayed at Branston – so close to the crime scene. Zeynep even knew Troy's room-safe combination! Everything is a trigger, especially for poor Zeynep. And, you have the revolver, now?'

'Yes. And I agree with you. Singh's revolver does not appear to have been fired, or crucially, cleaned recently. But forensics will confirm, presently. Mahatma concurs – Mr Singh did not have the opportunity to return the gun to the temple, and any accomplice would not have had the opportunity or inclination either. Mr Singh's revolver was probably at the temple throughout the incident and before. We will retain it as evidence, but it is unlikely the murder weapon. The boss was never convinced it was Mr Singh, but we must follow the evidence. He is, at the end of the day, the only person left alive from a locked room of murder victims.'

Jessica remembered Zeynep's suggestion of the mysterious accomplice being a soldier of the diplomatic bodyguard. At least half the soldiers forming the guard are Sikh and any one of them could have slipped into the temple, but then the gun has not recently fired. She decided not to throw that thought into the pot.

'*No accomplice* must mean Diaz is in the clear. And Sumer and Mr Singh are not working together.'

'We never said Diaz was an accomplice, Mrs Taylor. At this time, we are not accepting Singh's version of events and we are not fully satisfied with Sumer's account of his injuries. We are keeping all lines of enquiry open. Either man could have smashed the window. Sumer may have been making his escape, perhaps with Singh's assistance, when injured. And finally, Mrs Taylor, the Canadian's first lady to the High Commissioner to India has never been officially named as a suspect or a person of interest, in this case.'

'Please remember we are on the same team, Indira. Just check with *our* boss on that one.'

A frosty silence crept along the phone line.

'Ok Mrs Taylor – you win. Mrs Anderson left India immediately following the death of her husband and of Troy, claiming diplomatic immunity. We are therefore unable to eliminate her from our enquiries, and she remains a possible future suspect in this case. That information remains confidential – understood, Mrs Taylor? Confidential! Don't forget, being part of a team works both ways.'

'And don't you forget, Indira, it is I who had Mr Singh cooperate over the location of the revolver. I am doing my bit for the team.'

*

The two women sped north-west along the coast and then drifted east and inland towards the mountains and Wayanad

Hill Station. Zeynep mostly sat back on the rear pillion seat occasionally resting one hand on Jessica's shoulder when leaning into corners or overtaking lorries. The 500cc single cylinder engine coped well with the steep hills and tight bends, especially in lower gears. Their journey literally *stepped up a gear* once Jessica discovered the elusive fourth - by forcing up the foot selector lever with her toe, whilst simultaneously releasing the clutch lever with her left hand, crashing the constant-mesh gearbox into top. This *extra* gear released another fifteen miles per hour to the top speed.

Jessica purchased a vintage leather pilot's jacket and leather pilot's goggles for the adventure, Zeynep had her lamb's wool lined puffer jacket; both rolled and tied to the tool pouch fixed to the handlebars. Enjoying the cooler air, they avoided stopping to slip on the jackets as they headed higher into the mountains. Zeynep snuggled into Jessica's back, sharing body heat, and folding her arms around her friend's waist. The engine rhythmically throbbed. Zeynep drifted asleep as Jessica pulled the bike off the main highway and along cobbled sideroads towards a tea growing village in the direction of Wayanad Hill Station.

The mountain-mist laden cliffs and open countryside gave way to the main village street. Jessica slipped into the wake of a diesel-belching locomotive, towing a train of half empty goods wagons, pullman cars and third-class passenger carriages. The rails through the centre of the village ran along the stone cobbled street at an unforgivingly steep angle. The outskirts of the village nestled shacks and poor housing against the tracks, but closer to the centre jostled shops and food stalls, vying for custom from the slowly passing trains. Local passengers from the surrounding tea plantations and halts, situated downline, clung to the carriages, wagons, and locomotive footplates for a free ride.

Pigs scratched in the dust as the train approached, squealing, and running to safety at the last moment. Conversely, porters with barrows, hawkers, businesspeople, and travellers converged at the station to meet the train. Jessica called over a young barrow boy, laid out on his two wheeled, flatbed trolley.

'Excuse me. Is there a hotel close, please?'

The boy looked over his shoulder, assessing the ratio of barrows to goods and passengers delivered by the train.

'What standard of hotel do you ladies prefer, please? We have supreme luxury, fairly safe, shit, and dangerous.'

Zeynep woke, rubbing her eyes. Jessica smiled at the boy.

'As we are on an adventure, I think we will try the supreme luxury, please.'

'It is a problem. First, I must earn my 100 rupee transporting important goods to shops; I am in logistics. Only then, can I take you to the Victoria Station Hotel. A wonder of colonial plushness and beauty. But by then, this lot,' he gestured to the newly alighted passengers being crowded by the oversubscribed mob of porters, 'may have all the best rooms. What to do?'

Porter shook his head, perplexed and saddened by this seemingly insurmountable dilemma.

'What if I pay you a 100 rupee fee to take us, immediately, to the hotel? Could your colleagues handle the distribution of these important goods, without your supervision?'

'Yes. I think that is a workable solution. My guide/concierge fee is 150 rupee all found, including expenses incurred.'

'Deal.'

Jessica shook hands with the boy. He swung a leg over the motorcycle, sitting half on the front of Jessica's seat, and half on the petrol tank – squashing Jessica further back against Zeynep.

She revved the engine, depressed the clutch lever, and stamped the gear pedal into first. With the old clutch dragging, the bike lurched forward as Jessica compensated by decreasing the revs. The boy leant further back against Jessica's chest – she expected both passengers would soon slip-off to sleep. The boy signalled straight ahead, with the flat palm of his extended hand, as Jessica prepared for the uncomfortable journey ahead. After just fifty yards, the boy tapped Jessica's knee and directed her to ride through a set of railway-crossing gates, lovingly restored and relocated to the entrance of a beautiful, wooden colonial railway station building. Adjacent to the crossing gates stood a signal box, relocated as the security lodge. The boy and the security guard waved to each other.

The three climbed off the bike as a bellboy rushed to carry Jessica's leather bag and the two jackets.

'I must hand you over to my colleagues in hospitality. I hope you benefitted from my services. Our aim is to please.'

The boy took the 200 rupee note offered, bowed his head to the two friends, brushed his heart and stopped to collect his 50 rupee bonus from the gatekeeper.

*

The receptionist offered the couple a bedroom overlooking the railway tracks – the hotel popular with trainspotters.

'When do the trains stop running? We don't want to be kept awake all night.'

'Stop running madam? They never stop running. The train runs uphill past Victoria Station Hotel every Wednesday afternoon without fail. Friday morning, it will pass us again, on the journey back to the coast. Regular as clockwork.'

'Thank you. We will take the railway track view room.' The women grinned at each other. 'Two nights, please.'

'Dinner is served until ten-thirty. Snacks and drinks are available twenty-four hours, obviously.

'May we have a picnic breakfast for tomorrow, please? We are having a day in the countryside.'

'Of course, madam.'

The receptionist called for tea, booked-in an Indian couple and a German family from the recent train arrival, before sitting with the women to pour over a tourist map and itinerary for the following day in the locale and environs, including swimming in a freezing waterfall, a walk through a tribal mud-hut village, and tour of a tea plantation.

They freshened up and Jessica took a call from Indira, before returning to the hotel veranda, consisting of the old platform. There congregated most of the other hotel guests to watch the departing train clang, bang and belch the section of toothed railway, as the locomotive heaved towards Wayanad Hill Station; their trackside table reserved and shaded with a silk parasol.

They asked the waiter to recommend dinner from the menu, and shared a steaming plate of Kozhikode Biryani, rich with chicken, eggs, and lemon, accompanied by a separate dish of palak paneer – a buttery mix of spinach and cheese.

'I confirmed our location with Indira. Apparently, they are working through the UK Special Branch report on my date night recording. God, how embarrassing. I wonder if the shouting voice is yours or mine? I have already accepted the arguing voice is likely to be me, dreaming.'

'What, Jessica? What are you suggesting?'

Jessica shrugged.

'The only thing I am certain of, Zeynep, the shouting voice is either yours, or not yours; it is mine, or not mine. Did you shout at the children about something before the shots? Or did you have on Turkish television, perhaps?' Jessica shrugged again. 'Or what do you think? You glare at me whenever I ask these things – but that really is unfair; I am only the messenger – devil's advocate, at worst.'

'Jessica, I heard a woman shouting in Turkish, and I thought it was you. I don't know what else to tell the police.'

'Then don't tell anything different, Zeynep. Just tell them the truth. Did you hear the words shouted?'

'Not really. Something about killing them.'

'God! What, something about killing Cameron and Troy?'

'How should I know?'

'And definitely from the Anderson's room? Not from my room?

'I assumed from the Anderson's room. I may have been confused by the antihistamine overdose; I suppose.'

'Then the shots?'

'Yes, within a moment.'

'And the connecting door was shut and locked?'

'It was closed. I had just changed for bed; I felt very drowsy. But I don't know when the door was locked. I heard the shouting, as did Mr Singh and Sumer. Then the shots and soldiers bashing the doors and the window smashed. My bedroom door to the corridor is always locked. The connecting door is normally left unlocked. The Andersons and I both know to knock first, if either has closed the connecting door – to get changed, say, or have a moment together or whatever they got up to. But not normally locked.'

'Did you bolt it when you heard the shots?'

'No, I don't think so. Soldiers were battering my door and glass smashed from the balcony direction – I just dragged the children into the blanket drawer under the bed and climbed in with them. I felt sick with tiredness, from the antihistamine. I pulled the drawer closed by tugging on the slats of the bedstead. The next I remember is you pulling me out, then the soldiers attacking Diaz, Cameron and Mr Singh – with Troy dead on the floor. Or that is what I thought I was seeing at the time.'

Jessica sat on the seat next to Zeynep, pulling her tightly into a hug.

'You were so unbelievably brave Zeynep. Those kiddies are so fortunate to have you looking out for them.'

*

The couple enjoyed their day exploring the scenery of the Western Ghats, hundreds of meters above the dust and heat of the coastal plain. The day began cool; laden with mountain mist, which soon cleared to deep blue and cloudless skies. They motorbiked, hiked, climbed, and swam throughout the day, eating street food from the occasional roadside stall.

They visited a village of mud houses and drank tea with a tribal family. The mud brick, and reed-thatched house enjoyed no utilities, and divided into two rooms. One room housed two tall earthenware pots, full of rice and ragi millet, with a seemingly absence of any other belongings - other than the clothes they wore, two coarse blankets and reed bed rolls. Jessica purchased an ounce of home blended smoking tobacco, to thank them for their hospitality and sharing the tea. The head of the house accepted only a few rupees and gracefully declined pocket money for the children.

A fellow villager shouted from outside and entered the hut, talking in a local dialect of Malayalam. Jessica and Zeynep were ushered out of the hut and across the open village compound towards their motorbike. All the village adults assembled in a loose crescent between the huts and the forest edge. The men in an outer line, the women filling in the spaces behind their men. They held machetes and staves, with a few of the women armed with blackened cooking pans. Halfway between the forest edge and the huts stood a lone mountain leopard. As the villagers stared it down, some of the women threw rocks to land a few feet in front of the animal. The leopard raised a lip, flashing huge fangs in a snarl, looking from hut to hut, which housed the children and a few goats.

Jessica kick started the old motorbike, reluctant to ride away on the only piece of machinery in the village, which might help to confront the animal. As the single cylinder engine thundered into life, the leopard flinched and twisted slightly away from the village; the moment of weakness seized upon by the villagers whom, as one, ran at the leopard, shouting and screaming. For an awful moment, the leopard stood its ground. Jessica dropped the clutch and joined in the chase, horn blaring. The animal turned and sprinted for the safety of the forest.

*

'This kind of stuff follows you everywhere Jess?'

The two women lay on an oversized beanbag located on the hotel *platform,* staring up at the stars.

'Seems to.'

She took another drag on the huge spliff made from the tribal tobacco. They lay cheek to cheek, legs extended in opposite directions. Zeynep gave up on trying to hold the spliff, allowing Jessica to hold it to her lips.

'This trip away from home: you took a lover ...'

'Two lovers, actually. I made friends with the airline pilot.'

'... are a suspect in an international assassination investigation and fought with a leopard.'

'Seems so. Never a dull moment. I have never seen so many stars. Even high on dope, it is pretty spectacular. How many stars are there, do you think?'

'I know exactly how many stars there are. There are infinite stars, plus one.'

'If there are infinite stars, why isn't there an infinite amount of light? Why isn't night-time brighter than daytime?'

'You're weird Jess.'

'Thank you. If I introduce you properly to Sumer, will you actually do him?'

Both women took another drag.

'Sure. Why not?'

'Now, that is weird.'

'How so, Jess? You did.'

'But I don't suspect him of polishing-off half my adopted family.'

Smoking dope calmed Zeynep's mood swings. She lay silent for a moment, pondering Jessica's observation. She stopped trying to count the stars.

'I am still a woman Jess. Needs-must. What must not happen, and I am asking you to do everything in your power to help me please, I must not be arrested for anything, not even a parking ticket, until I officially have my new job. Can you help, please? Promise?'

*

The women packed the bike and took a leisurely breakfast, waiting to watch the train crawl slowly down the steep toothed section of rails towards the village station – the goods wagons now piled with a cargo of tea, destined for the coastal ports.

Both women wore their jackets against the cool mountain air, riding over the Ridgeback, between the Ghats, above thick rainforest, and down valleys towards the savannah grassland of Periyar National Park. They pulled into the tiger safari lodge well after dark. Reception took them straight to their luxury tents, complete with fully equipped bathroom, air conditioning for the daytime, and heating for the cool nights.

They ordered breakfast for early morning, to catch the first tiger jeep safari of the day. Zeynep ran the women a bath to share.

Jessica sent Jason a text to say she was safe, without mentioning the leopard, and tried to call Sumer, but he failed to answer. She then made the call to Indira.

'Hello Mrs Taylor. Is everything ok?'

'Yes, all fine. We had a lovely …'

'Are you alone?'

'Yes. Just Zeynep and I. Zeynep is running a bath ...'

'A bath!'

'Yes. Don't worry – I won't fall asleep or soak unsupervised, after last time.'

'Is Sumer with you? Have you heard from him?'

'No, his phone is off.'

'Are you on speaker phone?'

'No. I ...'

'I have Mahatma here for you.'

'Are you two still in the office?'

'Jessica. Mahatma here. Listen to me. We are driving up to see you.'

'Right. Can you say why? We are on a safari first thing.'

'We have a car here. We are driving up now. We will be there in four or five hours.'

'What? Why? What has happened? Shall I cancel the safari?'

'It is nothing to worry about. No, do not cancel. I do not want to spook Zeynep. In fact, best not mention to Zeynep that we are coming. We just need a sample of your voices, no big deal. No point in making her stress. You know how defensive she becomes. We will be there-and-gone before you know it.'

'You have my voice from the date night recording. And some heavy breathing, no doubt!' Jessica tried to make light, despite feeling deeply embarrassed by the situation.

'I will explain when we meet. One other thing, Jessica. Be careful.'

'A leopard …'

'Please Jessica, be careful. We now think you did not blackout in the bath. We now agree, somebody attempted to murder you.'

*

'You seen a ghost, Jess?'

Jessica slipped into the double roll-topped bath, opposite her friend.

'No, no. I am fine. Just that this is the first bath I have had, since I … blacked out. Plus, that was a long ride. It is ok for you, napping on the back.' The women smiled.

'Shall we finish the tobacco mix – help you to relax?'

'You have some Zeynep, I am cool. But thanks for thinking of me.'

'India's number one detective team have any breakthroughs? How did the voice checks go with London?'

Jessica shrugged. 'They don't tell me much, really.'

'All else ok?'

'Yeah. Absolutely. Looking forward to seeing tigers tomorrow.'

For the first time, she wished it was only Lidiri, with her dirty feet, hairy legs, and gaping chest wound, who shared her bath.

Chapter Sixteen

The women completed their usual bedtime routine, holding hands until Zeynep slept. Rather than sleep naked, Jessica wore a T-shirt; although she was not exactly sure how that might help should her assailant return. She listened to Zeynep's breathing regulate and waited for her to release her hand and turn over onto her side, long before she allowed herself to slip into a fitful sleep.

Through a fug of sleep, the noise of someone creeping in the room startled Jessica. She screamed as she woke, to see Zeynep loom over her.

'Jess! Easy. Everything is ok. Shush darling. I think our guide is here.'

'Sorry, I thought ... Sorry.'

Zeynep answered the wood-framed tent screen-door in her pyjamas as Jessica slid under the sheet and thin blanket.

'Good morning, ladies. Is all ok? You screamed?' Zeynep smiled and shook her head. He continued. 'I am your guide for the safari. Please, here is your breakfast.' He placed two dishes of curry onto the desk, covered with upturned plates. 'Also, some bread and jam. Please, I will see you outside in twenty minutes if you are ready.'

The guide took a moment to study the two women, before smiling and retreating outside.

'You can have my curry, Jess. I am happy with some bread and jam. How do you do that? Coconut and shrimp biryani at five in the morning!'

Jessica shrugged, shovelling another spoonful into her mouth. A bead of sweat ran from under her arm and down her side – following her fright on waking.

Both dressed in cargo pants and cropped tops under open long-sleeved shirts; meeting the guide sat in an open jeep, parked outside the lodge gates.

'I think you ladies will be lucky today. We transported two brother tigers from another reserve one week ago. They killed a tribal man foraging within the tiger's territory. Then, very sadly, they came into a village and took a twelve-year-old girl. We helicoptered them here, to break the man-eating cycle, hopefully. If it does not work, we will have to shoot them.'

'Are we in danger?'

'Potentially yes, all tigers can kill a man, obviously. They just prefer not to. But we will be fine in the jeep. The foresters and locals are on high alert. There is also a female with cubs in the area. She is worried about the brothers and is very defensive. But you are safe with me. And that is why you are here – to see these beautiful animals.'

'May I drive?' Jessica chirped in.

'Absolutely miss, you may not.'

As Jessica shrugged, and the other two laughed, a black Toyota Land Cruiser bumped along the dirt track towards them. Mahatma alighted the passenger side, leaving the door open and strode towards the group. Jessica noticed, for the first time, Mahatma's pistol, holstered under his linen jacket. Indira followed, pulling her cotton bomber jacket over her own firearm.

'Mrs Taylor! Zeynep. Good to see you.'

Zeynep looked between Jessica and the two detectives, taking a step back.

'We, just need … Sorry to interfere with your excursion.' Indira held up the mobile phone she pulled from Mahatma's trouser pocket. Jessica smiled at this seemingly intimate and uninhibited act. 'Just a voice sample, if that is ok?'

Zeynep looked to Jessica, who smiled back and shrugged. 'Sure.'

The guide sat back into his jeep to wait, as the detectives escorted the women to their own vehicle. They asked Jessica to read a Turkish children's rhyme into the iPhone voice recorder – once with a Turkish script and once with a printed English phonetic script. They turned to Zeynep.

'Wait. Am I a suspect?'

'Not at all Zeynep. You are still a person of interest. We are eliminating you from our enquiries. Hopefully, we can remove your *person of interest* status and let you go home. If …?'

Indira held up the mobile phone, again.

'When will this be processed, so I can go home?'

'London is four and a half hours behind us. It is nearly six o'clock here. If their forensic department starts at say nine o'clock and they open our email in eight hours, I don't know – maybe a few hours to run the test. Then …' Indira tailed off; Mahatma continued.

'Hopefully tomorrow, towards the end of our day, I would say, Zeynep. As soon as possible, I promise. Tomorrow is Sunday, but they have agreed to work on it over the weekend.'

Zeynep stepped back, taking Jessica's arm.

'If Zeynep is uncomfortable …?'

'Of course, Mrs Taylor. Zeynep, if you want to take legal advice and have a solicitor present, then we will completely understand and support you. We will have to ask you to accompany us back to Kochi. We have powers of arrest, under this circumstance, and shall, of course, release you as soon as you feel able to comply with our request.'

'Arrest? No way.'

Indira maintained eye contact.

'It is very much the nature of this investigation, Zeynep.'

Zeynep looked between the three faces, Jessica not understanding what Zeynep expected of her, other than to avoid arrest under all circumstances. Kindly Mahatma offered no alternative, nor tempered his junior colleague's stance.

'Is it worth providing the voice sample now, Zeynep? You will then have the weekend to arrange a brief, to guide you through the process.'

Zeynep nodded at Jessica. The police officers now looked between the two women.

Indira asked 'Why are you so concerned, Zeynep? You know the voice is not your own.'

Zeynep gulped and looked to Jessica again, for support.

'Zeynep has applied for a new Embassy job with the Canadian Diplomatic Service. She does not want to risk arrest, even for just a few hours over the weekend. She believes she should proceed carefully, cooperating with your enquiries, with a lawyer's guidance.'

'Au pair?'

'No. Admin.'

'Admin, Zeynep? Where, here in India?'

'No, in Turkey. Look, ok. I will do it. I will do the voice sample now. But I want it on record that I asked for my legal representative to have a copy and represent me in any further interviews. I will give you details on Monday.'

Zeynep grasped Jessica's hand, locking fingers, and pulling it to her chest. She cleared her throat and read the Turkish lyric.

'Thank you Zeynep. Good luck.'

'Indira! She does not need *good luck*! She …'

'Sorry Mrs Taylor. I meant good luck with the job application. We also want to have an informal talk with you both, please. Separately. It will not take more than an hour.'

'No! This is too much. We have an expensive tiger safari booked.' Zeynep broke loose from Jessica and stomped towards the guide, waiting in his jeep.

'She is under huge pressure. She is really wound up about the new job application and is terrified you lot will ruin it for her. Can't this wait until we are back in Fort Kochi?'

Mahatma smiled as if about to consent, but instead declined the suggestion.

'No Mrs Taylor. It won't wait. We will accompany you both on your safari. But then we must talk, separately. Here or at the station.'

*

The guide drove his four *tiger hunters* into the national park. He spoke more about the habitat, how the elephants, tigers, flora, and fauna are prioritised over locals and visitors. He explained how the national parks join by habitat corridors, allowing the tigers to roam the length of the country.

Jessica noticed how both Mahatma and Zeynep appeared agitated and less able to concentrate on the guide. Jessica was the first to spot the mother tiger, with small cubs, on the ridge of a low hill. The guide bounced the jeep off the dirt track and came to a clearing where they could watch and photograph the tiger streak. The cubs played as mother sunbathed in the rising sun, closing her eyes against the rays.

Without notice, tiger-mum leapt to her feet and ran into the thicker vegetation, cubs following with a faltering trot. Guide spoke.

'The males are nearby. They will kill the cubs and mate the female if they have chance. She is tormented by this risk, twenty-four hours every day. Perhaps we will see them.'

He drove the jeep through the clearing and into the forest in the opposite direction to the female's exit.

'Stop! Stop here!'

The guide brought the jeep to a halt on the bank of a dried stream. All faces turned to Jessica as she vomited, stepping out of the jeep as she did so.

'No miss. Please stay in the jeep.'

Jessica held up a hand to silence the guide, as she vomited again. She then waived Zeynep away, making her stay with the jeep as she moved behind a nearby Ghost Tree, pulling down her cargo pants. The guide stood on the tailgate, scanning the nearby forest. Hearing Jessica had finished, he sprinted over, ushering her back to the jeep, and immediately drove to the centre of a second clearing.

Jessica rinsed her hands in water Zeynep poured from a bottle, before rinsing her mouth and immediately vomiting again. Her face and neck reddened, sweat pouring. Zeynep helped her out of the long-sleeved shirt, her arms and top soaked. She sat on the shaded side of the jeep, against the wheel arch.

'That was embarrassing. Sorry.'

'A dodgy curry for breakfast?'

At the mention of curry, Jessica retched again. A small string of bile left her mouth, her stomach now empty.

The guide continued his scanning of the surrounding forest edge. An elephant ambled down the track, the mahout tapping his ankus goad in time to the strut of the beast. The mahout stopped to talk with the guide. The elephant fidgeted, flapping her ears. Oestrogen seeped from glands and ran in a sticky amber resin down her forehead.

'The forester has seen the male tigers. He can take my two guests on the elephant, to visit them. We cannot drive closer with the jeep.'

Jessica shook her head.

'Damn! I can't go.' She clutched her stomach as it cramped and rumbled.

'Let's get you back to the lodge, Jessica.'

'No! Absolutely not. You go. This is a chance of a lifetime. I can be just as ill here, as back at the lodge.'

'You can go with Mahout and Nelly miss. I will take your friend home and return for you on the main track.' He spoke with the mahout again, who wobbled his head in response.

'I better stay with you Zeynep,' Mahatma offered. Zeynep rolled her eyes.

'I really don't care what you do,' she muttered *'pig'*, under her breath.

Nelly reluctantly knelt to allow Mahatma and Zeynep to climb onto her back, both sitting side-saddle on the wooden frame designed to carry the forester's kit and produce.

'We can chat along the way, Zeynep. Indira – see if Mrs Taylor is well enough to discuss and confirm her movements on the fateful night, please.'

The guide laughed at Mahatma's suggestion of talking as they hunted the tigers – the ride promising to be a rollercoaster of crashing through the thick vegetation and uneven terrain, on a reluctant hostess.

*

Jessica felt stronger and calmer by the time they reached the lodge. She washed, sent her clothes for laundering, drank some water and only vomited half of it.

'Do you need a doctor, Mrs Taylor?'

'No. Thank you. I am feeling much better. I am just extremely sad to have missed the elephant tiger hunt. What exactly does Mahatma want to talk to us about, separately? Do you have more information about the shooting or the shouting voice?'

Indira sat opposite Jessica on low sofas in the shade of the tent veranda.

'The voice recording analysis has thrown up more questions than answers.'

'Go on.'

'To be honest, we thought the shouting female voice was yours Mrs Taylor – or Lideri's, if you see what I mean. Perhaps Singh and Zeynep were confused by the location, or the direction of the shouting and that it was unconnected to the shooting. We clearly heard you having a pop at Lideri just before the shots. Apparently, some of the 'Turkish' words were nonsensical, but it was clearly you. But your laptop Teams call also picked up the shouting voice – but not clearly. And the smashing window. Special Branch want to investigate further.'

Jessica shrugged. 'Sure. Zeynep and Mr Singh said it was me. But obviously I was not in the Anderson's room.'

'Singh heard the shouting; he thinks from the Anderson's room. But he did not actually say it was your voice. He did not know who's voice it was, or even that it was in Turkish, just that it was female and foreign. He was positive the arguing voice earlier came from your room, but not the shouting immediately prior to the shots. Zeynep said it was definitely you and definitely from the Anderson's room, and in Turkish. She said you shouted about killing, immediately prior to the shots being fired.'

'I honestly do not think Lideri …'

Indira held up a silencing hand. 'Mrs Taylor. What we are saying is we think a female was involved. London has identified you as the arguing voice. However, they have isolated the separate shouting voice in the background as your voice still argued upon your return from the balcony. At first, we were convinced all the Turkish voices were yours and not necessarily directly connected to the crime, but now we are less sure. You could not be arguing close to the microphone and shouting in the background at the same time. We do not now think the shouting female was your imaginary friend. But we still need London to confirm. We are aware that, off camera, you could have used a recording of your voice having your one-sided argument, whilst you were actually stood in the Anderson's room shouting.'

'Lideri is not imaginary! Well, not exactly. You make her sound … And anyway, why would I shout in Turkish to two English speaking men?'

Indira held up the hand for silence again.

'I am not here to help you prepare a defence Mrs Taylor. How has Zeynep acted since we released you both from hospital?'

'As mad as a box of frogs. And who can blame her?'

'Specifically?'

'Nothing specific. Just traumatised and scared, as am I, of being falsely accused. She is convinced it is Sumer. Perhaps with Mr Singh as an accomplice. Which makes it even stranger that she would sleep with Sumer, given the chance.'

The two women stared for a while.

'I didn't really mean that. I shouldn't have said. She is just lonely, I am sure. And fancies Sumer. He is cute.'

'But she fancies sleeping with a boy whom she suspects killed her friends?'

Jessica shrugged.

'I don't know. Ask her.'

'And she has fallen out with Diaz but is still in contact.'

'Really? I thought Diaz was blanking her.'

Indira tilted her hand, showing the comment sat in a balance.

'Murder is a capital offence in India, Mrs Taylor.'

'And?'

Indira shrugged.

*

Indira and Jessica heard Nelly trumpeting first, followed by a commotion of people shouting and Zeynep screaming. Nelly stomped into the lodge compound, throwing back her head and flapping her ears. She held her trunk high, trumpeting, eyes wide and wild with fear. Zeynep lay across the wooden saddle, gripping the rope tied around the elephant's neck.

Guides took to the three available jeeps and seconded the police Land Cruiser, speeding towards the forest. Lodge staff surrounded the stricken elephant as it circled, keeping them at bay. A mahout entered the fray from the staff accommodation, his goad casually resting against his shoulder – nonthreatening. He spoke gently, the receptionist translating for Zeynep.

'Please miss. Stop screaming. Do not try to get off Nelly, you are safer on her back.'

Zeynep's guttural scream soothed to a childish whimper. The Mahout broke eye contact with Nelly, looking around the group of staff as if taking them in for the first time. He told them to move back a little, and to avoid eye contact with Nelly. The elephant charged towards the mahout, stopping six-feet short and stamping the dusty ground. Without looking up, the mahout took a banana from his pocket, peeling and taking a large bite, before thoughtfully chewing and swallowing. About to take a second bite, he instead held it out for Nelly.

Nelly stepped forward, her own feet stamping close to the mahout's, taking the banana in her trunk and straight into her mouth. The mahout raised a single hand to the top of

Nelly's ear and guided her down to kneel, swinging onto her neck in one swoop. Resting the hook of his goad against the elephant's ear to keep her kneeling, he collected a whimpering Zeynep in one arm and swung her down to a second mahout who had then appeared, to assist.

Zeynep now safe, Nelly, carrying one mahout and escorted by the second, walked silently out of the compound towards the elephant shelter and the promise of a vegetable and fruit treat.

Chapter Seventeen

'Stop whining and tell me where they are Zeynep! Where are they?'

Jessica spat back an answer. 'Wait Indira! Just wait a moment. Christ!'

In the minutes following Zeynep's return, the lodge compound began to fill. First arrived two one-ton pickup fire-trucks. Shortly afterwards appeared three more jeeps carrying guides from a neighbouring lodge, with a pharmacist dressed in laundered whites and carrying a large medicine box. The pharmacist gave Zeynep a sedative injection.

'Do not put her to sleep! That is a direct order.' The pharmacist wobbled her head to Indira.

Within seconds Zeynep calmed, her breathing regulated. She closed her eyes as her head lolled to one side but stayed sitting with Jessica's assistance.

'Darling. Answer Indira. Where are Mahatma and Mahout?'

'It happened so quick. We were crashing through the jungle. Mahout stopped Nelly and pointed to one of the brothers lying in dappled sun, almost invisible, camouflaged behind just a few blades of grass - despite being huge, vast. Nelly jumped from foot-to-foot, stamping and trumpeting, ears flapping. And then it happened.'

She began to wail again. The pharmacist stepped forward, but Indira stopped her with the palm of her outstretched hand.

'*Then* what *happened*?'

'The second brother appeared from nowhere and must have dragged Mahatma from Nelly's back. He didn't even scream. He just disappeared, dragged into the undergrowth. Nelly spun around and Mahout tried to give chase, but then the first brother dragged him from the Elephant. He did scream, it was awful.' She sobbed into her hands. 'Nelly stampeded through the forest. I just held on.'

*

Indira nodded to the pharmacist. Zeynep lay down and instantly fell asleep to the sedation, as Jessica stroked her hair. One of the firefighters helped the pharmacist check the sleeping Zeynep for obvious injuries. The lodge compound continued to fill with ambulances, police, and forestry vehicles. An air ambulance landed on the dirt road outside the gate.

Indira and Jessica walked to the elephant stable. Tears poured down Indira's face and she did not want the accumulating police officers to see her crying.

'We are dating. Mahatma and I are dating. It took me ages to snare him, he is worried dating a colleague, especially a junior colleague, especially his junior partner. He calls me *his partner in crime*.'

'My God Indira. I had no idea. He is so lovely, and you are so cute. A lovely couple.'

Jessica moved to put her arm around the officer's waist, but Indira tensed, and Jessica released her – she continued to walk close, for comfort. The mahouts sat on their haunches in a close circle, chewing betel nut and spitting plumes of red juice into the dust. The working elephants stood chained in a meadow – the group circling a grieving Nelly, offering her pieces of fruit from the trough. The men stood on seeing the women; worry etched into their sun-baked, leathery faces.

They spoke a thick dialect from outside of Kerala, which Indira struggled to understand. One of the younger men spoke English, with a slight American cowboy drawl, from a youth spent in the cinema.

'Is there any chance …?' Indira did not need to complete the sentence. All the men's faces dropped to stare at the dust.

'Sorry miss. Perhaps if the tigers were chased away. Even if Nelly did spook them, they would have returned immediately afterwards to finish …, you know. But no, we do not think there is any chance the men survived. We are very sorry for your loss.'

Indira studied her notebook through a blur of tears, as if making notes. Jessica stepped forward.

'And we are very sorry for your loss, also.' The men understood her sentiment and nodded, even before the words were translated. 'And the tigers would have had no problem attacking the men and dragging them from Nelly? The tigers must have risked injury.'

The young man held an inquisitive frown and spoke to the group before answering.

'No miss. A tiger can, but is very unlikely, attack someone sat on the back of an elephant. Nelly is hormonal and the tigers would be very cautious around her, in case she attacked without provocation. Two tigers could attack a single elephant of Nelly's size, but unlikely. This did not happen today.'

'Definitely? How can you be so sure if you hardly know the brothers?'

The mahout talked with the oldest man in the circle and then with the mahout who had arrived to rescue Zeynep.

'Nelly has no tiger injuries. They would have ripped her flank and neck – just to reach the men. The men must have fallen from Nelly, before the attack. We were just talking – it is possible the policeman may have jumped down or slipped from Nelly. But something quite catastrophic must have happened for Mahout to fall. The young lady is very fortunate to have held on when Mahout could not.'

'From where this happened, would we have heard gunshots, from back here in the lodge?'

'Gunshots? Yes miss, we would. But despite what you may think, even Wild Bill Hickok would not have had time to draw and fire a pistol – let alone a detective policeman. If he had managed to fire a shot into the tiger, it is unlikely to have stopped the attack. It would be little more effective than a child's toy crossbow, against such a beast.'

Jessica nodded at the mahout. She avoided eye contact with Indira – wondering if shots could have fired immediately prior to the men falling off Nelly, not by Mahatma during the attack. Following her ferryboat faux pas, she decided not to offer Indira the benefit of her lack of experience.

'I will send one of the local officers to take a full statement. Thank you.' Indira nodded to the men, before leaving with Jessica. Jessica noted Indira walked slightly taller, back *in character*.

*

Jessica declined the offer of a lift back to Kochi with Indira as she still had Mr Singh's motorbike to return. Zeynep first begged to stay with Jessica and then bluntly refused the offer of a lift with Indira.

Indira telephoned the Inspector based at her station and they agreed she could not insist on Zeynep travelling with her. Zeynep had provided the voice sample required and they had no further grounds for arrest. Indira further suggested it may be advantageous to have the two women stay together; neither being left alone until the officers had had time to review all the evidence again. With Zeynep's unstable mental health and Jessica's recklessness and Lideri hallucinations, neither could be classified as safe to be left alone. Jessica walked Indira to the Land Cruiser.

'Mrs Taylor, we now have another enquiry ongoing – that of two men killed in a tiger attack. The National Park authorities may have some questions to answer. My first question is why did they not, at the very least, split the two brothers for relocation.' She shrugged and turned her face into the soft breeze, fighting back more tears. 'Not that it makes any difference now. Both brothers will be shot dead by tomorrow morning. I wouldn't be surprised if poor Nelly tramples the bones to dust.' She frowned and shrugged again. 'Although it is an ongoing investigation, I can tell you that *remains and items* have been recovered, confirming our worst fears.'

Jessica saw bags brought back to the lodge. Some loaded into the waiting ambulance, others into the back of a police Land Rover. Jessica did not envy the coroner performing the autopsy and trying to establish cause of death.

'Indira, why did you drive all this way, two of you, just for a voice sample? Why didn't we just send them remotely?'

'Mahatma is, was, very worried about you both. Perhaps he took his eye off the ball regarding his own safety. He is a deep thinker. He didn't say exactly what worried him, but I could tell he was close to making arrests. And the Indian Police Service does not work with evidence taken without supervision and randomly sent in by members of the public.'

'The voice samples themselves are important, though?'

'Yes, absolutely, Mrs Taylor. Every *I* need's dotting, *T* crossing. I need to sit with the uniformed Inspector and the Investigation Log. We need to consider the implications of hearing possibly two voices arguing and shouting. Perhaps we will have some news for you both on Monday.
'Mrs Taylor, please take good care of yourself and Zeynep. Local police officers will stay onsite until Monday, or longer, until the tigers are shot. May I ask, actually I insist, that you return to Kochi by Monday, please? And if Sumer should contact you, please tell him to call me, and also you inform me of the contact immediately. We have lost track of him. If you see him here or anywhere, you must call me and seek the refuge of a public space or protection of local police.'

'Of course, but I can assure you he is a harmless friend. Are you sure you are ok to drive?'

Jessica watched tears well in Indira's eyes as she nodded. Jessica pulled her into a hug and refused to release her this time, until the woman's sobs subsided.

*

Jessica and Zeynep rode the motorbike back to Branston Wharf Hotel for midday on Monday. Zeynep gripped Jessica tightly around the waist for the whole journey. She felt Zeynep's tears run down the back of her neck on occasions and other times she felt her snuggle into her back to doze.

As they pulled into the hotel forecourt, Sumer climbed out of an autorickshaw. He waved and both women waved back; Zeynep enthusiastically. Jessica turned to face her pillion, wide eyed with surprise, as Zeynep blushed deeply.

'Silly me, sorry, Jess. I thought he was waving to me. Probably not.' She continued to blush.

Jessica rode into a parking space and purposely dropped the bike hard onto its side stand, so Zeynep almost fell off, laughing.

Sumer spoke. 'Hello Biggles! You two summonsed, as well?'

Both women rolled their eyes in reply. Jessica lifted her leather flying goggles onto her head and loosened her pilot's jacket. Her face heavily lined and coated with dust and tanned by wind and sun. She lowered her voice.

'Where have you been Sumer? Your phone was off; Indira is after you again. Have you heard about Mahatma?'

'Don't worry, I have spoken with the *feds*. I was following the autorickshaw challenge through a race section and spent some quiet time camping. Your friend Indira is acting a little jumpy. I returned her calls when it was convenient, convenient for me! They released me from prison through lack of evidence – she needs to move on. And she can think again if she believes I will continue to provide alibis for my every movement! Nothing I do now is connected with those murders from days ago.
'So, what has happened to Mahatma?'

Jessica squeezed his hand for silence as they entered the lobby. A group of people gathered around the low table where Sumer and Jessica enjoyed their post lovemaking afternoon tea date. They looked at each other – Sumer blushed as Jessica smirked.

A uniformed police inspector sat in one seat; opposite sat a young woman in a sari – oozing confidence and gravitas. Indira stood respectfully to one side. Two uniformed officers stood at one end of reception. Mr Singh stood next to his concierge's lectern. He stood tall and proud, holding his ebony nightstick defiantly, bruises fading and his father's full sized kirpan visible from his belt, but without his pistol. Jessica ran to him and into a tight hug, dust from her clothes and hair billowing into a cloud around them.

'Good to have you back protecting us Mr Singh. And thank you for …' Jessica cleared her throat, '*lending* me your motorbike. It really is beautiful. Older, solid, powerful, reliable, and trustworthy – and still as handsome as ever.'

Singh acknowledged the comparison with a smile, inclining his head. He took a huge silk handkerchief from his pocket to brush dust away from Jessica's eyes, nose, and mouth, before lightly kissing the top of her head and using the handkerchief to brush dust from his own clothes.

The young woman rose to greet Zeynep, shaking hands.

'Good day Zeynep. My name is Mrs Vakil. I have been appointed by the Canadian Embassy to represent you, should you so wish. Let me confirm, please – the Embassy has instructed me, and they will settle my account, but I represent you. You alone. Shall we proceed?'

Zeynep nodded, her shoulders dropping with relief. She allowed Vakil to take her to a sofa in the far corner.

'Indira, I also need to make a call, before speaking to you. And I need to shower and change. I will be ready by the time Zeynep has finished her interview with the brief.'

'We have a time slot to Teams call Diaz Anderson. Can you please make sure you are back here within twenty minutes? It is like trying to herd cats, honestly!'

The women smiled to each other. Indira looked better than on Saturday, the day her lover was killed by the tiger. She must have managed some sleep and hopefully had Sunday away from the office, but she still wore a haunted look. Jessica glanced at the uniformed inspector, wondering if he was aware Indira and Mahatma were dating, or did he assume she was only grieving the loss of a colleague. Jessica was desperate to hug the poor lost police officer but knew any physical contact would be rebuffed by this stern professional.

Jessica retrieved her room key and asked reception to bring out drinks and biscuits for the groups of police and suspects, *by any other name*. As Singh left the room in one direction to check on his beloved Royal Enfield motorcycle, Jessica skipped up the stairs in the opposite direction. Indira made eye contact with her inspector and threw-up her hands in frustration.

*

Jessica sat naked on the edge of the bed, in the blast of the air conditioning, towel drying her hair.

'Jess, love, you have the camera angle set too high.'

Jessica studied her insert screen for a moment. 'No Jace, you can see my face perfectly well!'

'Like I said. Anyway, how was the motorbike adventure?'

Jessica thought for a moment, deciding to downplay events. She never really understood why Jason felt so annoyed when difficult situations arose around her.

'Not brilliant, Jace. I had a dodgy tummy and a couple of men were killed by a tiger near our lodge. But the journey itself was fun. Except Zeynep – she is a nightmare. One minute she can't get close enough to me, especially in bed, the next minute she is screaming at me for harbouring the murderer of her friends.'

'Explain, exactly, the bed situation. Will you?'

Jessica crinkled her nose into a smile. 'You really are a sick puppy, Jace, you really are. Ok, so every night we have a naked pillow fight, and the loser has to seduce the pizza delivery-boy.'

Jason returned the grin. 'Now I know you are making it up. You would never eat pizza when curry is available.'

'Anyway, I know which team Zeynep bats for. She blurted out how she fancies Su…, the suspect from my office. One minute she is accusing him of murder, the next she is ask…, telling me she might try to seduce him. Weird.'

'That isn't right Jess. Nobody could be friends with someone they even faintly suspect of helping or being a murderer. She is either seriously messed-up or doesn't really believe he did it. In fact, she must be certain – otherwise she wouldn't be able to sit in the same room, let alone the same bed. And if she is coming to you for comfort, she obviously does not think you are covering up anything.'

'She can't know anything, for certain. None of us can. Even the police are flaying and floundering. The detective in charge of this end of the investigation has gathered all the suspects, or *persons of interest*, together downstairs for some kind of brainstorming session. I guess she is hoping someone will contradict a tiny morsel of something else that is said. Just looking for any inconsistency. And although Zeynep is all over the place emotionally, she is sure of exactly what happened to her and the kids during the shooting – even though she was drugged, almost to sleep. As you say, she must be messed-up. Or she thinks she knows who the murderer really is.'

'No, it would definitely have to be more than just *thinks she knows*, to be prepared to take a suspect to bed.'

'Yeah, Jace. I guess you are right, as always.'

Jessica stood, purposely allowing her husband to see her naked as she walked slowly to the laptop to disconnect the Teams call and prepare for the meeting downstairs.

*

Jessica walked slowly down the stairs towards the assembled group. She hesitated twice, stopping on the stairs to catch her thoughts. Her hair still damp, she wore an oversized shirtdress, with wide candyfloss-pink and white vertical stripes. She bought the dress especially for her India trip. Jason said how she looked like a beach deckchair and then made a rude comment about wanting to stretch-out on her. She thought again about his comments regarding Zeynep. She untied and retied the material belt, glancing at the matching canvas slippers – the left mostly pink with a white flash, the right mostly white with a pink flash. For a moment, the group thought she would head back up the stairs.

'Mrs Taylor? Jessica? When you are ready, please. We are waiting.'

'Sorry Indira. Yes of course.'

Jessica took her seat.

Indira formally introduced everyone to the meeting – herself, Jessica, Vakil, Zeynep, Singh, Sumer, the police inspector, and Diaz on the hotel television screen.

'Thank you all for attending.'

Sumer threw up his hands and flopped further back into his chair. 'Like we have a choice! I have been released from prison through lack of evidence, but you are still harassing me!'

Jessica leant forward to take his hand and reassure him, but Zeynep already took his other arm. Indira continued.

'It has been a terrible week for us all. And I, again, offer our deepest sympathy to you Mrs Anderson for the loss of your husband Cameron and your friend Troy, and to you Zeynep for the loss of your friends and colleagues. As if that wasn't awful enough, we are now investigating the death of my colleague Mahatma and of Mahout and the possible assault and attempted murder of Mrs Taylor as she bathed.'

All other faces turned to Jessica – only Zeynep and Indira failed to make eye contact, both had their own teary eyes to contend with.

Sumer squeaked with surprise. 'Mahatma dead?'

Diaz spoke. 'So, all you have accomplished, so far, is two more victims. Well done.'

'We are not saying the new cases are murders. But under the circumstances …'

'Under the circumstances! Jesus Indira, it is like the blind leading the stupid.'

Indira visibly tensed, she was not about to have Diaz, having runaway back to Canada, cast doubt on Mahatma's integrity and capabilities.

'Mrs Anderson! Let me assure you, Mahatma has brought this investigation close to conclusion. And as you have kindly put yourself to so much trouble, by bothering to turn on your laptop from seven-thousand miles away …'

The inspector held a hand to calm his junior colleague. The room fell into an awkward silence.

'Ok. Let's start again. We will look at the timeline for the night. You will each concentrate and comment as we go. You will each, respectfully, stop me to add any detail, regardless of how insignificant or minor you believe the information to be.'

'Sorry. I need to take this call.' Zeynep clasped her mobile to her ear and walked towards the quiet corner of the room, nodding to herself.

'Zeynep!'

Indira shouted across the room. Zeynep continued a short conversation, before slipping the phone back into her pocket and walking back to the group, offering no further apology.

'Indira, I wish to say something.' Zeynep cleared her throat and nodded towards her lawyer. Mrs Vakil stood.

'My client is subject to diplomatic immunity, from the Canadian government. She cannot answer your questions.'

'What?' Indira spat the question. 'She was the fucking au pair …' the inspector cleared his throat, but Indira continued, 'and now it is too late to claim anything. This is a live investigation!'

Vakil produced a ream of documents from her briefcase, sorting and placing them into two neat piles on the coffee table – originals and copies.

'My client, Zeynep, now holds the position of Personal Assistant at the Canadian Consulate to Turkey. That position is covered by the international laws of Diplomatic Immunity. She has not been charged with any crime in India.' Vakil continued to add documents to the piles – the confirmation of the job offer, and other legal documents. 'Please have your legal people review these documents, but I assure you, they are in order. We have an embassy car waiting outside.'

'No Mrs Vakil. I am not going yet. I wish to stay here, with Jess and everyone.' She checked her phone and raised a hand to silence her brief.

Jessica looked first to Zeynep – she had a look of fear on her face, a young woman out of her depth. Then Jessica glared at Diaz on the screen.

'You did this Diaz! You arranged Zeynep's new job and immunity. Don't you want answers to who killed your husband?'

'Don't you judge me Jessica, you provincial little tart! Why would we support that lot? My husband died in their country, in their care! They botched the investigation and will probably hang some innocent man, one day. Zeynep – leave now, with Mrs Vakil!'

Zeynep turned away from the screen, tears ran down her face.

'I am not having this shit. I will arrest you all if I must!'

Indira took a few steps towards reception; the uniformed officers sprang to attention. She kicked over a chair, before returning to the group.

'Ok. This meeting continues. I will take any silence from Mrs Anderson or Zeynep as incriminating.'

'My client, and I suspect Mrs Anderson, are not permitted to waive their diplomatic immunity. You must apply to the Canadian Foreign office. My client, Zeynep, is not trying …'

'You, sit down and shut up! Or I will have you arrested for obstruction.'

The inspector held Indira's wrist for a moment. The dynamic between the two police officers reminded Jessica of Mahout and Nelly. Mahout may have been in charge, but only with the tacit agreement of the oestrogen dripping cow elephant. She pulled her hand free and took several deep breaths.

'Ok. I am going to work through the events of that evening. If anyone holds back information, I will have them prosecuted!' Indira glanced at Zeynep. 'To the best of my ability and with the full force of the law.' The last comment to pacify her senior colleague. 'Mrs Taylor, you are on the team, you start.'

'Sure. Umm. Well. I had been video calling my husband. We had supper *together* and then, you know, drifted off to sleep *together*. I woke when I heard a noise on the balcony. I saw … someone.'

'You saw me Mrs Taylor.' Singh spoke. 'We waved. I can absolutely confirm Mrs Taylor returned to her room. I continued my rounds. After a short while, I heard someone, Mrs Taylor I assumed, perhaps arguing with herself in a foreign language.'

'It was a dream. Zeynep was arguing with Lideri in my dream. It isn't always a dream, as such, with Lideri. But Lideri cannot argue with other people. Obviously. Because she is dead and everything. So, it must have been just a dream.'

'But that could have been you arguing with Zeynep, as Lideri, Mrs Taylor?'

Jessica looked up at Indira and shrugged. She looked to Zeynep for confirmation but received no response.

Jessica continued. 'Yeah Indira. I guess so. I think I fell asleep in my room. Then I was woken by two shots.'

'I heard the shots.' Sumer spoke. 'At first, I was sat right here. I was hoping Jessica might fancy an ice-cream or some air.' Zeynep let out a long sigh. 'I wandered to the pool, waiting for a response from Jess. When I heard the shots, I tried to run towards her room, but the soldiers were everywhere. I ran back to the pool and climbed up the balcony structure, until this oaf battered me with his nightstick. You could have killed me, man!'

'I did hit you, Sumer. Because I thought you were escaping from the Anderson's room. We all know about your family's gripe with the protesting farmers and the Canadian High Commissioner supporting them. I heard a woman shouting in foreign and then the shots.' Singh looked back to Indira before continuing. 'Then I broke the double-glazed window to the Anderson's room. There was no key inside the balcony door, so, if you never found a key on Sumer, perhaps he wasn't escaping. Or perhaps he threw it somewhere.'

Sumer scoffed. 'Yeah, like the police wouldn't have found it, or noticed a key missing and not accounted for. And anyway, Mr Security Expert – there is no access to the balcony door lock from outside and you said the door was deadlocked – from the inside!'

'Let me continue, son. I am not explaining myself to you; your snooty caste means nothing to me! I climbed in, seeing the men and the blood. I smelt the gunpowder discharge. Mr Anderson was groaning. I opened the bedroom door to the soldiers, tugged on the locked connecting door to check on Zeynep and the children, but was then *arrested*.' Singh sub-consciously raised a hand to his bruised temple.

'I rushed out of my room when I heard Diaz screaming.' Jessica continued. 'I went into Zeynep's room with the soldiers. I found Zeynep and the children in a drawer under the bed.' She looked to Indira.

'You apparently knew where to look.'

'I, I just guessed. I'd had a dream … Look, I just guessed. I helped Zeynep and the children. They were all drugged. I saw a knife with a brass handle in Zeynep's hand and pushed her away. Zeynep tried to defend herself with Troy's pistol. She fired it as I kicked it away. Then I slipped and …' Jessica shrugged.

'I had no knife!' Zeynep shouted, before Vakil laid a restraining hand on her arm.

Jessica stood and took a position between Indira and the inspector, facing the screen.

'What is the story behind the DNA Testing, Diaz?' Indira moved to guide Jessica back to her seat, but Jessica refused. 'Mahatma made me part of the team Indira, remember? He trusted me, so should you. Diaz?'

'Zeynep took some swabs from the children. Standard practice, no big deal.'

'But the other swabs? Zeynep took swabs from herself and Troy.'

'She shouldn't have done so. She is just a stupid little girl with some *daddy syndrome.*'

'But what did the tests show Diaz? Is Troy your children's father?'

Diaz burst into hysterical laughter. 'Troy? You are joking! Troy was a good friend of mine and was Cameron's best friend. We don't all have to be unfaithful to our husbands to have fun, Mrs Taylor!'

Jessica ignored the slight. 'Speaking of which, Zeynep, why would you want to sleep with Sumer – the man you think might have killed your father fixation?'

'Oh, for God's sake Jessica!'

'My client …'

'*Shut up!*'

Jessica, Indira and Zeynep shouted at Vakil in unison.

Zeynep continued. 'I am not interested in your sloppy seconds, Jessica! You with your brown heritage and slutty western ways. You are just a melting choc-ice, melting in the Indian sun. Say goodbye to your brown shag and run home to your forgiving, perfect husband – who can't even satisfy his wife!'

Jessica bristled at her comments about Jason. 'You are prepared to shag my seconds because you know, *know*, he isn't the murderer! Only two people *know* Sumer is not the murderer! Sumer, and the murderer!'

The room fell silent. Zeynep fell back into her chair.

'Zeynep. You need to shut the fuck up and go to the embassy with Vakil.' Diaz spoke calmly, but with authority. Jessica walked to the screen.

'You knew!'

'If, *if,* Zeynep has anything to answer for, she will answer to the Canadian courts. I have not worked all my life to protect people around the world, to have one of my own hanged in some black hole in Calcutta! Zeynep – go to the embassy.'

Jessica turned to Zeynep, her back to Diaz.

'You drugged the children and then yourself, with antihistamine. The children were already safely in the drawer, before you killed the two men.'

'You are talking rubbish, Jessica. How did I get back into my room; there were soldiers everywhere? Singh tried the connecting door; it was locked from the Anderson's side, with the key blocking the keyhole. The balcony door was deadlocked from the inside. The bedroom door was deadlocked from the inside. And motive: why would I want to kill Troy, my father as I once thought, and Cameron, the man who secured my Canadian citizenship? You are mental! You have been trying to blame Troy all this time, but his gun was only fired once. You were trying to blame who I had believed was my dad - now you are blaming me. You are deranged Jess, deranged.'

'A man raped your mother and gave her AIDS. Yeah? You were infected and AIDS wiped out your whole family over two generations. Troy and the Andersons plucked you from wage slavery and saved you. Yeah?'

'*Yeah* Jess *yeah*! Exactly. I have less motive to kill Troy and Cameron than anybody in this room – your poor little rich-shag Sumer, your fighter-without-a-cause Singh. You and your *blame everything on dead Lideri*. I love my family! I love my brother and sister!'

'Zeynep!' Diaz shouted again.

'And why did you spend so much time tracking down Zeynep originally, Diaz? Or did Troy know exactly where to find this motherless girl? Did Troy call in a personal favour from you and Cameron, after abandoning Zeynep's mother? My God yes! You know exactly what the DNA results prove, Zeynep. You know the skeleton in the Anderson cupboard.'

Diaz spoke again. 'Zeynep, you little cow, stay silent. I mean it.'

Indira found her voice.

'Zeynep, Mrs Anderson. This is probably your last opportunity to help clear this mess. If you know anything to help convict or clear individuals – it really is morally imperative that you say so, now.'

'Troy did work with my AIDS charity. Yes, I think he may have nominated Zeynep for our support. So what?'

'And you didn't question that nomination, Diaz? Then you offered Zeynep a position in your own household and you and your husband went to huge efforts to secure her Canadian citizenship, even falsifying a national security reason not to identify her real father. Finally, as the net is tightening around your husband's murderer, you secure Zeynep a last-minute job, which comes with diplomatic immunity.'

'We look after our own Jessica. You might not have a loyal bone in your body, but I do!'

'No Diaz. Ever the diplomat first lady, you are being very selective with your answers. Troy called in favours, big favours on behalf of his little girl, as he then thought. Some would call these favours blackmail, perhaps; you certainly could not refuse him. He called in favours to secure his plum job as diplomat bodyguard to his friend. What *hold*, did he have over Cameron? What *favours* did you both owe him? Did he know something? Is that the same *something* you are holding over the Canadian authorities to have Zeynep face trial in Canada, rather than India? In Canada where the trial can be held in camera for security or official secrets reasons?'

'Jessica, you are way off track. Yes, I want a fair trial without anyone facing the death penalty and yes, Zeynep is one of my own. But I am not interfering with the law. Too many cosy Agatha Christie books and C.A. Larmer detective stories, love. Zeynep, why are you delaying? Let these amateurs play parlour games alone. Please get moving.'

Zeynep glanced at her watch, phone, and the hotel door.

'Diaz is right, Jess. You still have offered no motive and no opportunity. The brainy half of the good-cop-bad-cop partnership is feeding tigers. You have nothing. Lideri will pop in to see you later, to tell you how useless you are. Until then, give it a rest.'

On hearing the flippant remark about Mahatma's death, Indira stood to her full height, before stepping forward to slap Zeynep hard across the face. Singh stood and raised a defensive hand, his kirpan slipped to the floor with a clang. He reclaimed it, slipping it into his belt with his ring of master keys, including a single *fits-all* heavy brass mortice lock key.

'Opportunity? Wait!' Jessica spoke again. 'The brass handled knife that you held. It wasn't a knife, was it Zeynep?'

'I never had a knife, Jessica. That was one of your slanderous rumours.'

'No Zeynep, it was not a knife, my mistake. It was a big brass key, to the connecting door. You locked the door from your side, but placed the key back into the Anderson's keyhole, during our struggle. When did you first become aware of the actual, physical key in the lock, Indira?'

Indira shrugged. 'The first mention of that key in the Investigation and Evidence logs was some time after the scene was secured and Scenes of Crime had moved in.'

'Did the key have Zeynep's prints and DNA …'

'Of course, it did! I may have handled that key several times – it was the connecting door key to my room! And the gun Jess? What about the gun? I have never owned a gun and where have I hidden it? It would hardly flush down the toilet, would it?'

Jessica glanced at Indira.

'We checked the toilet, Mrs Taylor, obviously.'

'And Zeynep's toilet? Or just the Anderson's?'

Zeynep had appeared nervous throughout the meeting, but her face now contorted with panic.

'Don't be ridiculous. The loo barely flushes the children's wipes. It wouldn't flush a whole gun!'

'You didn't need to flush a whole gun, Zeynep, did you? Only two empty shell casings.'

Indira spoke. 'But only the one shot was missing from Troy's ammunition magazine.'

'True Indira. Where could you have found your own supply of replacement ammunition Zeynep? Remind me again, what was the combination to Troy's room safe? Your birth year in reverse, wasn't it?'

Diaz spoke again. 'Zeynep, Mrs Vakil, I want you both in the embassy car, now. You, Mrs Vakil, are looking at a bonus or at losing your job. You decide.'

Vakil stood, grabbing Zeynep's arm and pulling her up. Jessica stepped forward, slamming the palms of her hands into Vakil's chest, winding and sending her flying back into her seat.

'What was the hold Troy had, still has, over you Diaz?'

'Nothing! We were all friends. With the children and Zeynep, we were one, big family.'

'Families have skeletons, Diaz. Let's assume the DNA tests are all correct. Two tests fully shared their DNA codes – they must have been the children: same mother and same father. Zeynep told me Troy was one of the tests and she was the other. Zeynep is the half sibling and is not related to Troy, or Troy is the children's father and, still, not related to Zeynep.'

'I have already told you Jessica. I told you Troy is not my father.'

'No Zeynep, but Cameron is, isn't he? You said your mother was raped and the rapist gave her AIDS. You thought Troy was her lover and your father. But it was Cameron who raped her and gave her *you*. Troy was her lover, but gave her AIDS, which infected you and killed your family. Meaning the children really are your half-siblings!'

'This is ridiculous!' Diaz's voice trembled.

'Perhaps Cameron boasted or confided to Troy about the rape. Cameron must have panicked when he first realised his victim had AIDS – he could easily have contracted the disease – that would have been some rough justice. Perhaps Troy found out from the investigation that followed. Perhaps Troy discovered he had AIDS after the affair, or he knew all along. But in any event, he used that knowledge about the rape to gain support for, whom he wrongly assumed, was his daughter. When you told him, Zeynep, about the illicit DNA test, he must have been as surprised as you at not being your father.' The room remained quiet. 'Motive? You murdered Troy, the man who gave you and your family AIDS before abandoning you all. You also murdered Cameron, the man who raped your mother. You only knew who your father really was for a few hours – now you really are an orphan.'

*

Singh heard the commotion first. He and the two uniforms moved to the lobby door as two Turkish navy infantry soldiers marched in, followed by a naval officer and two suits. Canadian embassy staff, having waited in the embassy car, bustled around this unexpected entourage, shouting.

Zeynep stood.

'Indira, Inspector. I am claiming the protection of my embassy. I am still a Turkish citizen; I have dual nationality with Canada and Turkey.'

'What?' Indira spoke. 'But …' She gestured towards Vakil and Diaz.

'I am being persecuted by the Indian and Canadian governments. Turkey is providing me with protection.'

'In that case, young lady, I am arresting you for the murder of Troy and Cameron Anderson.'

Zeynep looked towards Vakil.

'Um. Actually, no. My client is the subject of Diplomatic Immunity, as directed by the Canadian foreign office, regardless of where Zeynep seeks protection.'

The Turkish, white helmeted soldiers moved close to Zeynep, pushing Indira away.

'Zeynep! What happened to Mahatma? Please.'

The Turkish suits tried to usher Zeynep away, but she stood her ground.

'Wait. Mahatma was going to arrest me. He all but told me so. He knew the shouting voice in the background of Jessica's date night video, from immediately prior to the shots, was not Jessica's voice, as compared with her date night video voice. All he had to do was check my voice against the video, to prove it was me. But I had to stay free of arrest and charges until my job offer and promise of Canadian diplomatic immunity was confirmed, which it was, earlier this morning. If I was in custody prior to qualifying for immunity …' She shrugged.

'You killed him?' Tears now streamed down Indira's face.

Zeynep shrugged again. 'No. The tiger killed him. All I did was hit him once with a lump of firewood. And Mahout. I really had little choice. Think of it as self-defence.'

Indira took a step back pulling out her pistol. Jessica shouted and stood between Zeynep and Indira. Singh stepped forward, pushing Indira's hand, with the gun, upwards. A shot discharged, hitting the redundant punkah fan.

Chapter Eighteen

Indira remained in the hotel lobby, sitting with Sumer and Jessica. Singh was keen to return to work and took up his post at the hotel gates. Jessica Teams video called Jason and introduced him to her companions.

'It all kicked off a moment ago, Jace.'

'There's a surprise. Are you ok? Everyone ok?'

'Yeah. There was a shot fired, but none of us can remember by whom – perhaps Canadian or Turkish security, who cares.' She winked at Indira. 'It turns out our murderer was Zeynep, alone. What you said about her wanting to shag Sumer here is what got me thinking.' Sumer blushed and bowed his head. 'Look at you Mr Heartthrob. All the girls queuing up to have their piece of you!' Jessica playfully grabbed his shoulder and shook him.
'And it was premeditated. Totally planned. She helped herself to a fistful of ammunition from Troy's safe, drugged the kiddies, hiding them in the drawer, before having it out with the two men. Troy must have been sideswiped when she accused Cameron of being her father; Troy knew of the rape but had always hoped and assumed that he was Zeynep's father. Diaz probably knows more than she is saying, but Troy must have previously used the rape of Zeynep's mother as leverage over his friends. Firstly, he secured himself a cushy job, then he brought Zeynep into the fold. But between them, the two men were responsible for the rape of a vulnerable young woman and infecting four people with HIV/AIDS, three of whom died.

'She unlocked my connecting door and unbolted it from her side, to muddy the water, and replaced the spent shells and hid the casings to confuse things.'

'I don't understand. Why not just allow the finger to point at Troy?'

Indira answered.

'Troy had no reason to kill Cameron, and even less reason to kill himself. No motive. We would have been looking for someone else immediately. Perhaps we would have found residues on Zeynep's clothes, but by discharging Troy's gun during the struggle with Mrs Taylor, she has an alibi for any residues. From beginning to end, she added layers of confusion. We did not have any evidence to charge Sumer and Singh, but she was happy to kill Jessica in the bath for trying to defend them.'

'So that *was* an attempt on your life? Christ Jess!'

'Later love. All the time, Diaz knew Cameron and Troy's dirty little secrets and did her best to extract Zeynep to Canada for trial. She is scared Zeynep will blurt out her mother's story to defend her actions and avoid the noose, publicly exposing Cameron as the rapist.'

'The final piece of theatrics was unnecessary. Speaking to my inspector - Zeynep entered India on a Turkish passport, as a Turkish citizen. Even if the Canadians invoked diplomatic immunity, we would have deported her back to Turkey. I think this is why Diaz was so keen to have her protected by the Canadian Embassy - so they could whisk her back to Canada before any Indian notice was issued, which would have resulted in her deportation to Turkey.

Perhaps Zeynep was worried about being kidnapped by the Canadians and forced to Canada for trial.'

Jason spoke again. 'And the Turks won't prosecute?'

'Not a chance love. Since the Canadians recognised the Armenian genocide in 2004, Turkey has been looking for a way to snub Canada without causing an international incident. What better way than offering immunity to the suspected killer of the Canadian High Commissioner, who had been in position in Turkey during the diplomatic row over the genocide. And Zeynep still has her hold over Diaz and the Canadians. If they make a move to have her extradited, she will start singing about the behaviour of their martyred hero, family guy, and now suspected rapist - the deceased High Commissioner to India. She has them over a barrel. I have no doubt she will wangle a cushy Canadian job in Turkey, through NATO or the diplomatic service, or at least get pensioned off from her new job as PA – final salary, no doubt.'

'And the two guys killed by tigers, near your lodge? And the food poisoning? You know I can see when you are hiding something from me, Jess.'

After shaking Sumer's shoulders, she had taken hold of his arm and locked fingers, pressing his hand firmly into her lap. She suddenly pushed his arm away and cleared her throat.

'Yes, you have me there Jace, sorry. I just don't like to worry you. The bad tummy was coincidence, I think. If I had been well enough to ride the elephant, perhaps it would have been me in danger. But you know me and curry, sometimes I just cannot refuse something exotic, spicy, and served to me on a plate.' She glanced at Sumer and turned scarlet. 'Like the smell of curry and everything, you know. But yes, the men were also killed by Zeynep. One was the mahout, a witness. One was the detective inspector. Zeynep, probably correctly, thought he was on to her. She had to delay any arrest until after Monday morning, when her job offer and associated diplomatic immunity was finalised. Mahatma was a bright and capable police officer. Kind, caring, lovely, and cute as a button.'

A single tear escaped Jessica's eye and ran down her cheek; Indira nodded in the background.

'She hid the kids in the drawer, had it out with the two men – accusing her father, Cameron, of raping and impregnating her mother. And her mum's boyfriend, Troy, of infecting her with HIV/AIDS, which Zeynep still has to live with. She pulls Troy's gun from the holster, shoots him through the heart and turns the gun on Cameron. She then collects the spent shell casings from the floor, reloads the gun, rushes into her own room, locks the connecting door and waits to be rescued.'

'Then what?'

'Clutching the key, she uses the children as a shield, scraps with me until she is covered in blood and has fired the gun, before yanking at the connecting door, to cover her slipping the key into the lock. All in plain sight. Yeah? What seemed like a chaotic string of random events was actually carefully orchestrated by Zeynep.'

'Firing the gun, and all that blood, masks any residue from her having shot the men?'

'Exactly, Mr Taylor.' Indira spoke. 'My people have been back into Zeynep's room. Mahatma's, well *my* mistake, was not to check Zeynep's toilet for evidence, only the Anderson's. In the U-bend of Zeynep's toilet was five surplus live rounds and two empty casings. Troy kept the ammo in his room-safe and she worked out the combination. He always used her birth year in reverse for four-digit pin numbers. Further down the drain is a filter to catch items before the hotel macerator. In that filter we found disposable gloves and a disposable apron of the type Zeynep used to change the children. They have been washed by the toilet waste too many times for forensics, but my guess is she wore them to reduce the blood splatter when shooting Troy at close range.'

'How did she manage to overpower the two men on the elephant?'

Sumer raised his head and looked towards Jason, too coy to make eye contact with his lover's husband.

'My people own an elephant sanctuary. Not as grand as it sounds. Just a couple of retired mahouts from our estate, a few retired working elephants, and a couple of wild orphans. Anyway, I have been on an elephant's back as it faces down a tiger. This is a battle of the titans. The tiger can kill an elephant, but must first fight five-tonne of screaming, stamping and jabbing foe. Trapped or defending young, a cow elephant can kill or mortally wound a 200kg tiger. Zeynep and Mahatma would have felt at sea in a bathtub during a storm, whilst sat on the back of Nelly. Earlier Zeynep said she hit Mahatma with a lump of wood, stored in the forester's pack. She would only have to dislodge Mahatma. Once on the ground, it would be a race to see what killed him first – the tiger or the marauding elephant. I doubt Mahout looked behind him, I am sure Zeynep could have spared Mahout's life, but she killed him anyway.'

'It doesn't compare with the death of the men, obviously,' Jessica reached for Indira's hand, 'but Zeynep also leaves behind two shot male tigers and a traumatised elephant. Quite a trail of death and destruction.'

'And all because her daddy was a rapist.'

'Christ Jace, that is deconstructed to the extreme, even for you! I realise nobody actually thought, for a single moment, that Lideri or I was in anyway involved, but being in the frame gave me a little flavour of the trauma and pressure the other suspects were under. Poor Sumer here, Mr Singh, even Diaz – although she was complicit in withholding evidence. And poor Troy was both a suspect and a victim for a while.'

As one, Jason, Indira and Sumer cleared their throats and leant back in their chairs.

Jessica continued. 'What? You must be joking! Nobody suspected me! Sumer? Indira? Jason!'

'Of course not, darling. Not much, really. Hardly at all. I admit my heart stopped when you were accused of shouting at the men in Turkish in the Anderson's room, especially as you had disappeared from my view, and I had heard you arguing with Lideri earlier.'

'Charming! While I was arguing with Lideri just before the shots, Mr Singh heard Zeynep shouting at the men. He never said it was me, he admitted he wasn't sure. Only

Zeynep pretended it was me. It is a good job Special Branch applied due diligence and isolated the shouting voice in the background from my arguing voice on the video! Good job Mr Singh has more faith in me than my own husband – I bet you would not have accused your friend Priti of murder!'

Jessica saw Sumer squirming out the corner of her eye. He touched her arm, but she shook him away.

Indira mumbled, sounding embarrassed, 'Special Branch were not actually able to identify the shouting voice. The recording quality wasn't …'

Jason continued speaking over her. 'That is not what I said Jess.'

'Fuck off, Jace.'

'You need to come home Jess. Please. I am begging you. The dog is missing you.'

Jessica caught Jason's eye and they both smiled. Jessica quickly cancelled the smile into a sullen pout.

'Yes Jace, soon. Sumer needs to get back into the project after a week away. I want to spend some time with him, in the office I mean. Then I will move to the Airport Hilton for a couple of days, booking a flight. I could do with the rooftop pool, safe in the clouds, and some partying with the airline crews. You know me Jace, I like to unwind; I don't want to bring my problems home.'

'But you are coming home?'

'Sure.'

*

Jessica stayed in the lobby. She stared into middle distance, taking and downing the beer directly from the waiter's hand. The second glass of beer barely placed on the table before she also drank half of it.

'I think that was mine.'

The voice startled Jessica. She jumped, spilling the beer, and laughing.

'Shit Sumer, I forgot you were still here. Sorry.'

Jessica allowed Sumer to pull her over to him, resting her head against his chest.

'Don't say shit and stop apologising. Not polite.'

Jessica scoffed.

'Jason seems a nice guy.'

'Excuse me? Who does?'

'Sorry, Mr Taylor seems a nice guy.'

'Stop apologising. Not polite. Yes, he is great, lovely. I love him so much, sometimes it hurts. But he can be such a dick. I can't believe he suspected me, even for a moment!'

'And you can be a bit stuck-up, sometimes. Didn't the Turks give you a medal for shooting someone?'

'Don't you start. He is my husband; it was out of order. Anyway, you're the one with a crossbow in his room! I never suggested to Indira that you might have shot Mahatma and Mahout off the back of Nelly, did I?'

The couple sat in silence, sharing the remains of the second beer.

'What happens now?'

'Straight afterwards, we crash back into work and get the project on track. You need to make a good impression, Sumer. I am talking just a few days - let's nail it! Then I make my way to the airport, home, and out of your life. I am not looking for validation or any kind of response, so please do not comment – but without knowing me, you would not have faced the gallows. Jason tells me off for getting into trouble and I do realise I take others along for the ride.'

'*Straight afterwards* what?'

'Straight after I crash the kitchen here and make you an English Sunday roast lamb, with mint sauce, Yorkshire pudding, bread sauce, and all the trimmings. The chef will allow me if I make him a plate. Are Sikhs veggies?'

'No, not as a religion, and thank you. Best not tell my Brahmin parents that I now eat meat – on top of all the other things I now do.' He blushed. 'I need to pop home to change.'

'No hurry, I will be in the bath, waiting. Bring an overnight bag and work suit. I need to ensure I am definitely not leaving behind a virgin. I still can't believe my husband doubted me.'

'I told you to stop calling me a virgin! But I agree, you should double check, Mrs Taylor.'

'And you didn't suspect me of committing murder Sumer? Not even for a moment?'

'Nah Jess. You're alright. If I did, which I am not saying I did, would you withdraw your invitation to stay tonight?'

'Yes Sumer, I bloody would!'

'In that case Jess, I never suspected you, not for a moment. And I assume you never suspected me either?'

Jessica shrugged. 'Who even keeps a crossbow in their room?'

Printed in Great Britain
by Amazon